The
Lost Treasure
Of
Bogus Bluff

Dan Bomkamp

Lovstad Publishing
Poynette, Wisconsin
Lovstadpublishing@live.com

ISBN: 0692490981
ISBN-13: 978-0692490983
Previous ISBN: 0615779360

Printed in the United States of America

Cover design by Lovstad Publishing

This book is dedicated to my Dad, Mike.

Our time together was short but what time we had...

...we used well.

Other books by Dan Bomkamp:

Adventures of Thunderfoot

More Adventures of Thunderfoot

Thanks, Thunderfoot

The Gosey

Big Edna

Voyageur

Lost Flight

Tag

Whiteout

Spirit

Thanks

As usual I want to thank my friend, fellow author and publisher Joel Lovstad for his help editing and producing my books. It's always good to have another viewpoint.

I want to thank Brandon Maloney and Brett Felton for appearing as Andy and Trevor for the cover photo.

And thanks to my childhood friends who explored Bogus Bluff with me those many years ago. We went into dark places and emerged unscathed.

The Lost Treasure Of Bogus Bluff

Chapter 1

The cast was perfect. The small floating lure, a silver and blue Pop-R, landed within two feet of the treetop that was lying in the water next to the riverbank. The river had carved the bank away inch by inch over the years. Finally there wasn't enough sand and dirt holding up the tree anymore and it had fallen over into the water. It was a perfect hiding place for a predator like a bass or northern to lie in wait for their next meal. The lure was immediately caught up by the swift current and carried toward the branches. Andy Benish twitched his rod tip and the lure made a splash with its dished-in face. Andy let the lure sit on the water as the ripples from the twitch radiated out from it. Suddenly the water exploded as a large smallmouth bass engulfed the lure. Andy snapped his rod up to set the hook and the fight was on.

"Whahoo!" he whooped as the fish turned its side to the strong current and bulldogged out towards the middle of the river. He put pressure on the rod and the fish jumped from the water once, twice, three times.

"Looks like a good one," his friend Trevor Ingalls said from upstream where he was fishing a similar lure next to a similar treetop.

"It's a dandy," Andy said. "He's fighting like a real champ."

Andy played the fish carefully as he was only using light line and after several more jumps the fish slowed down. The runs were shorter and shallower. The fish had used up a lot of energy and it was tiring from the pressure Andy kept on the line. Andy skillfully led it up to the edge of the sandbar and stepped down over the edge into the water and grabbed it by the lip. He lifted up the 18 inch fish and showed it off to his friend.

"Wow, a beauty," Trevor said smiling.

Andy admired the bronze fish with dark bars running down the side of its muscular body. He carefully took the hook from its mouth and put it into the water. He held it by the lower lip and glided it back and forth through the water letting oxygen flow over the fish's gills until it began to move its tail back and forth. Then he let loose of it and watched as it glided down into the deep water.

"Pretty," he said, "real pretty."

He walked over to the flat bottom boat that was pulled up onto the sandbar and laid his rod and reel over the seat. Then he opened the cooler and grabbed a bottle of water from it. His pal Trevor was fighting a fish that could be a twin of the one he'd just released. He smiled as he watched Trevor skillfully play the fish, land it and turn to show it off.

"What do you think?" Trevor asked holding up his fish.

"I think you had a good teacher," Andy joked.

Trevor just smiled and released his fish. Then he walked over to the boat and sat down on the edge next to his best buddy.

The two boys were both in their junior year of high school. Andy had grown up in the small town just downriver from them and had been fishing in the river ever since he'd learned to ride a two wheeled bike. Trevor had moved to town the year they were freshmen and the two had become friends soon after school had started. At first Trevor had little interest in the outdoors and the river, since he'd come to town from a big city where they didn't have such things. But it only took a few weekends with Andy for him to begin to love the river and the woods and all the fun things they could do there.

They were similar in many things. Both had single parent families and lived with their mothers, which was something they shared with many other kids at school. Both were hard workers and good students. They both had part-time jobs half a block apart. Andy worked at the local hardware store and Trevor worked at the grocery store on the other side of the big parking lot that also served two banks, and a clinic. Andy played football and baseball while Trevor wrestled and played baseball.

Andy looked over at his friend who was drinking from his bottle of water. Trevor was a typical wrestler. He was about 5' 10 and slim but very muscular. He was a good looking kid with short dark hair and brown eyes. He always had a smile on his face and very rarely had anything bad to say about anyone.

Andy was a little taller and also well built but a little heavier. He was not fat but not as skinny as those wrestlers always seemed to be. He also had dark hair which he kept at a medium length and had bright blue eyes. The two of them were good natured and easy going which is probably the reason they became such good friends when they met.

Their freshman year they'd been in four classes together starting with Physical Education first period in the morning. They'd been partnered up with each other for archery class and had soon become friends. Andy knew he'd found a crazy new friend when Trevor waited until their teacher wasn't looking and launched an arrow high into the air which landed nearly a block away in the town swimming pool. It wasn't long and Andy invited Trevor to go out on the river with him to do some fall fishing and the next thing they knew they were duck hunting together and then they deer hunted together. From then on, they seemed to be together most of the time.

"Those were two nice fish," Trevor said. "I wonder if those brush piles down there are holding any?" he said nodding downriver to a couple of trees lying in the water.

"Only one way to find out," Andy said.

They got up and stepped off into the water and waded quietly down to the trees. The water was just waist deep and the soft sand bottom of the river was great for wading. Trevor kept going and began casting to the lower tree while Andy stopped at the upper one and made a cast.

Andy's bait had hardly landed when the water exploded and a huge northern engulfed his bait.

"Oh no! A northern grabbed it," he shouted.

Trevor laughed. "Good luck with that," he said.

The fish took off up river and Andy put as much pressure as he dared on the line. The fish surged toward the middle of the river and suddenly his line went slack.

"Dang, he got my bait," Andy said shaking his head.

Trevor was grinning as he watched the action. "I'll sell you one of my spares," he said.

"I've got more, thanks pal."

Andy began wading back just as Trevor hooked into another smallmouth. This one wasn't very large and the fight was over more quickly. He cast again to the brush and this time he got a white bass.

"Can't beat dumb luck," Andy said from the sandbar.

Trevor released the fish and cast half a dozen more times and then waded back to the sandbar.

"Whew it's getting hot," he said as he sat down on the edge of the boat.

"Yeah, let's take a swim since we've got our shorts wet anyway."

They were both already barefoot and shirtless, so they dove into the deep water below the sandbar and swam and goofed around for a while. Then they waded back up onto the sandbar and lay down in the warm sand.

"I'm sure glad you showed me all the things to do on this river," Trevor said.

"I knew you'd like it once you tried it," Andy said smiling.

"It's a great place."

They lay there for a while and suddenly Trevor looked over at Andy.

"Look up there on that big hill. See that black place? That looks like a cave."

Andy looked where Trevor was pointing. There were seven huge bluffs that bordered the north side of the river along this stretch and this was the second last one in the string of bluffs. It was very tall and very steep on the front side that faced the river. He also saw what looked like an opening in the face of the rock cliff.

"That might be Bogus Bluff," he said.

"What's with it? Is it a cave or just a black rock?"

"I'm not sure," Andy said. "I've heard Gramps talk about it. I think it's a cave."

"Cool, we should go and look at it," Trevor said.

"We're not exactly dressed for climbing up that hill and crawling around in a cave," Andy said.

They were barefoot and in shorts. They did have tee shirts with them and flip flops, which were probably not very good for climbing.

"Yeah I guess you're right. It looks like it's up there a long way. We'll have to bring some proper clothes one of these times and look at it," Trevor suggested. "Why is it called Bogus Bluff?"

"I'm not sure. I heard something about buried treasure once, but I wasn't paying attention very good. Let's ask Gramps when we get home."

Chapter 2

The boys fished several more treetops on their way back downriver to the boat landing. They spent a lot of time fishing each treetop so it took long enough that it was pretty late by the time they got the boat loaded up. They decided to go see Andy's grandpa the next morning. Andy dropped Trevor off at his house and then backed his pickup and the boat into his driveway and went in for a bedtime snack.

Trevor pulled up in front of Andy's house about twelve hours later in his jeep and honked and Andy came running out wearing his usual summer attire, shorts, a tee shirt and flip flops. Trevor was similarly dressed.

"To Gramps?" Trevor asked.

"To Gramps."

As they turned the corner by his grandpa's two story house they saw Andy's grandpa sitting in the back yard next to his vegetable garden in a lawn chair.

"He's probably having his morning coffee," Andy said smiling as he watched the old man turn and wave to the boys.

Andy's Grandpa Benish was a local "character". He always had a yarn to spin and was always on the lookout for a chance to pull a fast one on some unsuspecting victim.

"Hey Gramps, what's up?" Andy said as they walked up.

Andy stooped over and hugged the old man.

"Good morning boys. I'm just sitting here contemplating all of those weeds that are growing in my rows of vegetables. I think when I've finished my coffee I'm going to try to pull some of them. Of course you know how my sciatica acts up. Once I bend over it's real hard to get straightened back up. I just hope that I don't cripple up right in the middle of the garden. I'd hate for the ambulance people to trample my vegetables when they come to haul me out to the hospital. I'll probably have to take a break every few minutes, but if I work at it long enough I probably can get it done in a week or so."

He sighed heavily.

"Maybe I can just crawl into the garden and sit between the rows," he nodded, "Yeah....that might work."

Trevor grinned at Andy. "Maybe we could help," he said.

"Oh I wouldn't want you boys to use your precious time on my old garden. You've probably got much more important things to do today. There must be some girls to chase or some fish to catch."

"We'll make you a deal Gramps," Andy said. "You tell us about Bogus Bluff and we'll weed while you talk."

"Bogus Bluff.....why the interest in that place?" Grandpa asked.

"Oh no real interest," Andy said. "We were out on the river fishing yesterday and saw what we thought was a cave entrance and I remembered that once a long time ago you were talking to someone about Bogus Bluff. We were just curious."

"Well you came to the right place, I'm an expert about Bogus Bluff," the old man said. "You might as well start right here in front of my chair on those radishes while I tell you."

The boys walked to the garden and squatted down by the rows of radishes and began pulling weeds.

"So do you want the 25 cent cheap tour or the $2 full lecture?"

"Well we might as well get the full story for all of this labor," Andy said grinning.

"Ok," the old man said. "Well to really understand this we have to go back to the Pleistocene. Are you familiar with that?"

"It was the last ice age," Trevor said.

"That's right it started about two and a half million years ago and ended about 10,000 years ago. The entire top half of the world was covered in ice. That means Russia, Europe, Asia and all of Canada and about half of the upper part of the United States. There were thousands of square miles of ice that was about a thousand feet thick. Here in Wisconsin the ice extended down to about Baraboo. It never got down as far as where we are here, which is why we have all of these hills and valleys. The upper part of Wisconsin is just as flat as a pancake and that's because the glaciers moved over the land and ground everything to gravel. Then for some reason the climate changed and about 11,000 years ago the ice began to melt. It took a long time but when it was all done, the Great Lakes were formed, all of the Canada Shield lakes, all of the lakes in Wisconsin and Minnesota and this river valley. There was a huge inland sea called Lake Agazzi that covered most of Canada and the northern part of Minnesota and North Dakota.

In our part of this world, the Wisconsin River valley was part of a huge lake that was formed by the glacial melt. Everything we see here looking at this valley was under water."

"Even the hills?" Andy asked.

"The hills were formed by the lake. If you think of the hills like the sandbars in the river that are there now, that's how the hills were formed. They were deposited by wind and wave action and sediments borne on the wind dropped into the water and were piled up creating huge piles of material that eventually solidified into limestone, and sand stone and other hard deposits. As the sediments piled up the pressure on the lower parts was enormous and caused the loose sediments to turn to stone. Then as more water accumulated up in the middle of the state, a natural barrier was created that acted like a dam. It finally overflowed and when it did, the whole dam collapsed and the result was an enormous flood of millions of gallons of water flowing down the middle of the state and eventually down this valley. The ancient Wisconsin River was already here and the flood connected this lower part to the upper parts that were formed by the flood. When the water came down this river valley it scoured the fronts of those big hills that lined the valley and eroded the front of them away. That's why many of these big bluffs are gradually sloped at the back side, and a sheer cliff on the front. Of course you have to remember this took many years, probably a thousand years or more."

The boys had stopped pulling weeds and were sitting on their haunches enthralled by the story.

"I think you have all of the weeds in that spot," the old man said.

"Sorry we got too interested," Trevor said.

They moved down the row and the old man continued.

"I suppose you're wondering why that flood has anything to do with Bogus Bluff. Well you have to realize that the tops of those hills were once under water and that's why Bogus Bluff is there.

When the hills were formed there were different kinds of minerals that were piled up to create them. Some of those deposits were piles of sand that turned into sandstone. Some deposits were calcium that turned into limestone. And others were the makings of hard rock that turned into dolomite. Once the tops of the hills were exposed after the water began to recede, the cave making process began.

Rainwater picks up carbon dioxide as it falls through the atmosphere. Then when it soaks into the ground it picks up even more carbon dioxide and becomes a weak acid called carbonic acid. As it seeps through the rock it will begin to dissolve limestone. It does nothing to hard rock or dolomite but the limestone is weak and easily dissolved by acid.

Usually there's a sink hole someplace on the hill top that collects rainwater and as it seeps into the ground a tiny bit of limestone dissolves and that little crevice eventually becomes a hole which becomes a cave. Of course this takes a thousand years or so to happen.

"So Bogus Bluff was formed by rain?" Andy asked.

"Yes over many centuries."

17

"That makes sense," Trevor said. "I was wondering why that hole in the hill was up on the hill so far."

"The thing with Bogus Bluff and most other caves is that they're much larger than they appear at first. I'm sure the first people inside had no idea of how many passages and tunnels there were. When I was a kid some of my buddies and I went up there and we crawled around in the thing for a whole day and I don't think we saw it all."

"No kidding? So you've been there?"

"Oh many people have been there over the centuries. There's quite a legend about that cave," Grandpa said.

The old man got up and moved his lawn chair to the next section of the garden.

"You might as well move over here to the onions and beans," he said motioning to the rows.

Andy and Trevor moved over and started pulling weeds from the onion rows.

"So how did the cave get its name Gramps?"

"Well boys that's another story that will take a while."

"We've got all day," Trevor said.

"Ok, well, we have to go back to the Civil War days when the counterfeiters were up there making fake, or bogus, $20 bills."

Chapter 3

"We might as well move over to the tomatoes," Grandpa said as he carried his chair down along the edge of the garden. He settled back and started his story. "What do you boys think was the main way people traveled back in the 1700's and 1800's?"

"Probably on horse or horse and wagon," Andy suggested.

"How about you Trevor?" Gramps asked. "What would your guess be?"

"I'd say horse too, or walking."

"Nope, they did walk from place to place and they did use horses for short trips, but they didn't use wagons. What do you suppose they used for roads? There were no roads for the horses to travel, let alone wagons."

Andy face lit up. "Rivers, they used boats and canoes."

"Go to the head of the class," Gramps said.

"That makes a lot of sense," Trevor agreed.

"In those days rivers were the highways of the time. That's why there are so many towns and cities along rivers. They started there many years ago and grew from little river settlements to cities and towns we now have."

"Starting sometime around the Civil War there was a gang of counterfeiters and river pirates that infested the Wisconsin and upper Mississippi River. They operated from Portage to Prairie du Chien and robbed travelers and merchants."

"There were pirates on the river?" Andy asked.

"Yes, pirates are found by almost any water, be it ocean, lake or river. A lot of people traveled by river also, so it was a good place to find people to rob."

"They also had a counterfeiting operation making fake $20 bills. That counterfeit operation was done in Bogus Bluff, hence the name Bogus, meaning fake or counterfeit. These cutthroats terrorized the people using the river for many years.

But in 1878 government agents were closing in on them. The story goes that the government agents trailed a couple of the counterfeiters to Bogus Bluff and watched them climb the hill and disappear into the cave. They left spies behind and rowed their boats back downriver to Boscobel and gathered a huge posse to attack the bad guys.

When they came back up the river the counterfeiters learned they were coming from their own spies along the river and got ready. The lawmen spread out in front of the hill and began climbing up to the entrance. Of course they ran into rattlesnakes and a very treacherous climb up a very steep hill, so it took them a long time to get up to the entrance. Dozens of them raided the cave only to find not just one tunnel, but three. They had no idea which tunnel led to the counterfeiters so they split up and began searching.

"There're really three cave tunnels?" Andy asked.

"Yes there are three main tunnels in the cave. Later many cross tunnels were cut by Cornish miners but we'll get to that part of the story later."

"So one group went down the left tunnel and followed it for a long way to find it came out on the west side of the hill about a quarter of a mile from the entrance. If the counterfeiters knew they were coming they could have escaped down that tunnel.

The group that went down the right tunnel found that it started out allowing a man to stoop over and walk down it. But within a hundred yards it began to narrow down both in height and width. In no time the government men were crawling on their bellies through what seemed to be an endless tunnel."

"How did they see?" Trevor asked.

"They had lanterns and candles, I suppose. There were no

flashlights in those days. It must have been pretty scary crawling on your belly knowing that bad men were possibly ahead waiting for you and probably carrying guns."

"Especially if you were carrying the lantern and they were hiding in the dark. You'd be a pretty good target," Andy said.

Grandpa nodded, "So the guys who went down the right tunnel finally came to the end and crawled out of a hole that was nearly on top of the hill, overlooking the river. They had been going uphill all the while but it had been so gradual they didn't know it. This was yet another way the counterfeiters could have slipped past them."

'How about the middle tunnel?" Andy asked.

"Well those lawmen didn't have far to go. That tunnel only went twenty yards and then narrowed down to an entryway into a room. The room was about the size of a small bedroom and was probably enlarged by the counterfeiters so they had a place to work and sleep. The ceiling was blackened with smoke from candles and torches and there was a lot of stuff left behind but no counterfeiting plates for making the bills."

"So they got away?"

"No, they got away from the guys on the hill but there were several deputies who were left at the river who were guarding the boats and they saw the counterfeiters sneaking down the hill to boats they had hidden down the river bank a little way west of the lawmen. One of the deputies ran up the hill as fast as he could go and raised the alarm and all of the lawmen hurried down and off they went downriver chasing the counterfeiters.

They caught up to them several miles later and arrested them. They found fake bills on them but not the printing plates. It was figured that they'd dumped them into the river to get rid of the evidence. They took them back to Boscobel and they were tried and sent to prison. Three of them were the most notorious counterfeiters in the country at the time."

"Wow, that's a good story Gramps," Andy said.

"Oh that's just the beginning of the legends of Bogus Bluff. I think we should move over to the cucumber rows and one of you should run up to the house and get me a little more coffee and a couple of sodas for you guys."

Trevor jumped up and took the old man's coffee cup and trotted over to the house. Gramps moved his chair down the garden a little way and sat back down.

"You and Trevor get along pretty good eh?" he asked.

"Yeah he's my best friend Gramps. He's a heck of a good guy."

"I think so too. I'm glad you two are friends. Sometimes grandpas get worried about their grandkids doing stupid things. I don't worry about you guys."

Just then Trevor came walking back with a cup of coffee and two sodas balanced on a plate filled with fresh oatmeal cookies. "Your wife thought we looked like we were hungry," he said grinning.

"Well, I know I could use a cookie," the old man said.

The boys sat on the ground and they ate cookies and had their sodas.

"Well, let's get started on those cucumbers and I'll tell you about the first treasure that's hidden in Bogus Bluff."

The boys looked surprised and began pulling weeds.

"We're all ears," Andy said.

Chapter 4

"**H**ave you boys ever heard of a fellow named John Jacob Astor?"

"Yeah, he was on the Titanic when it sank," Andy said. "I remember that name from the movie. He was a rich guy who went down with the ship."

"That was John Jacob Astor IV. He was the great grandson of the man I'm talking about. Astor was an immigrant from Germany who landed in the United States in 1794, just after the American Revolution. He was a clever businessman and found out right away that there was a lot of money to be made in the fur trading business. The market for furs in Europe was flourishing. Beaver pelts were worth a huge amount of money for fancy hats and fur coats. Astor saw that there was a fortune to be made and got in when the business was just beginning. Furs had been traded for years here in the States but there was a limited market. When Europeans found the quality and quantity of the beavers here the market went wild and old John Jacob was a shrewd businessman. He saw the potential for making a lot of money shipping furs off to Europe. So he began trading with trappers in Montreal and shipped furs to New York and then across the ocean. Some time later the Great Lakes area opened up to fur trade and Astor was right there to get in on it. The Great Lakes were some of the main routes of travel and Astor set up business in the region. He began the American Fur Company and in no time he was one of the wealthiest men in the country. He was the first millionaire in the United States. As he expanded his business he started a trading post at Prairie du Chien in what would someday be Wisconsin. Of course that was a prime place for his trading post because it was right on the confluence of the Wisconsin and Mississippi rivers. And, as we've already mentioned, rivers were the mode of travel.

In the early 1800's Astor had major ports on the Great Lakes and used the Fox River to get to the area that is now Portage. His agents would travel up Lake Michigan to Green Bay and then up the Fox. At Portage the Wisconsin River is only about 2 miles overland from the Fox and they carried their canoes and boats across this land to get to the Wisconsin and down to Prairie du Chien. That's how the city of Portage got its name, because it was a portage from one river to the other.

One spring in the early 1800's, Astor sent his buyers on a journey to deliver enough gold to Prairie du Chien to buy furs for the next year. This group loaded the gold and supplies into large canoes and began their journey up the Fox. At Portage they built a large flatboat and transferred the gold to it. Then they started down the Wisconsin. The early part of the journey went without incident. But the peaceful journey didn't last. When they got "within 5 days paddle" of the Mississippi, they were attacked by local Indians and the men carrying the gold to Prairie du Chein were defeated in battle. Most were killed but a few escaped by swimming under water until they could surface near tall grass where they hid. The Indians steered the raft to shore and removed the gold and then set fire to the raft and let it go down the river, where it eventually sank. The survivors waited until it was safe and then found their way to Prairie du Chien and reported that the Indians hauled the gold up a very high hill with an opening in the front of it and hid the gold in the cave."

"We're about 5 days from Prairie if you're paddling a canoe," Trevor said. "They hid it in Bogus Bluff?"

The old man nodded and smiled. "Right you are Trevor. They took many canvass bags of French Napoleons. They were a 20 Franc coin that was used often in those days and they weighed just a little shy of 1/5 ounce. At today's price of gold they'd be worth about $350 apiece. Give or take a buck or two."

"Holy smokes," Andy said. "So there were sacks of them?"

"I don't think anyone knows exactly how much money there was and I'm sure the story has grown over the years, but if you figured they had enough money to run the trading post for a year, it must have been quite a bit. Trappers brought their furs to Prairie from all over the area and there were hundreds of men who were trapping beaver, otter, mink and muskrat. So there were many dollars worth of furs to be traded. Astor was a multimillionaire by that time so he surely had plenty of money to work with to buy more furs."

"So it's never been found?"

The old man grinned. "You're getting ahead of the story."

"Sorry Gramps, maybe we should start on the potato patch?"

The old man nodded. "I was just about to suggest that."

They moved down the garden and Gramps started again.

"Astor continued in the fur business for many years and died in 1848. Before he died he expanded his holdings into land, buying huge tracts of land on Manhattan Island, which today is New York. He had holdings all over the United States. His net worth when he died was around $20 million dollars. If that was converted to today's dollars he would have been worth $110 Billion dollars.

"Whooie," Trevor whistled. "that's amazing."

"He spread his wealth around donating millions to build the New York Public Library and many other important buildings. He was a generous man and his heirs were also very generous.

His great grandson was indeed a passenger on the Titanic. When it was sure that the Titanic was going to sink, Mr. Astor and his butler dressed in their finest eveningwear and stood by letting woman and children take the places in the lifeboats. It was said he stood his ground and remained a gentleman to the end as the ship sank around him."

The boys were spellbound by the story and had stopped pulling weeds. They were sitting on the ground listening.

"We're never going to get this garden cleaned up with you two sitting there like that," the old man said.

The boys grinned. "Sorry, we were just thinking of all that gold and how much it might be worth today."

"Well, that gold is only part of the treasure," Gramps said.

"What? There's more?"

The old man nodded. "Oh there's lots more."

Chapter 5

"All we've got left to weed is the strawberry patch," Gramps said. "Trevor, run up to the house and ask my wife for a bowl and you guys can pick us some strawberries while you weed and we can have some for lunch."

Trevor sprinted up to the house and Andy began weeding. When Trevor got back he joined Andy in the garden and the old man continued his story.

"In the early 1800's the lower part of the Mississippi was still controlled by the Spanish. One of their explorers, Hernando De Soto was one of the first to explore the river after first finding it near present day Memphis. That's why we have a town called De Soto near here. He traveled the entire Mississippi and mapped the whole area. Because of him the Spanish had a lot to do with the expansion of this part of the country.

There were Spanish outposts in Canada and they used the

Great Lakes and Fox and Wisconsin Rivers the same way the French traders did, as their highway. The Spanish treasure was a shipment of gold doubloons that were being sent to New Orleans via the Fox, across the portage to the Wisconsin and then down the Wisconsin to the Mississippi and on to New Orleans.

The story goes that when the Spanish soldiers in charge of the loot were in the same general vicinity as Astor's men had been, they were attacked by a band of Indians on the river. They battled hard but soon found themselves outnumbered and defeated. One lone man survived by swimming under water until he could surface and hide from the Indians. He made his way downstream and hid in the brush and observed the Indians carry the gold up a tremendously high hill and watched them disappear into a cave. He made it back to civilization by traveling down the river until he met friendly people and eventually made it to his destination, minus a fortune in gold. They were carrying the payroll money for the soldiers in New Orleans so it also must have been a sizable amount of money. From what I've read, a Spanish Doubloon was worth about the same as those French Bonaparts that had been stolen from Astor's men."

"So the Indians just dumped it in the cave and left it or what?" Andy asked.

"Well, that's the million dollar question isn't it?" Gramps answered. "It's said that they hid it in a side tunnel in the cave and sealed it up so no one could find it."

"Why steal it if they weren't going to spend it?" Trevor asked.

The old man shrugged. "No one knows if they spent it or not. That's the mystery. They might have taken it out later and no one knew about it, or they may have all been killed in another battle and never got back to it. No one knows for sure. But the story isn't over yet."

The boys grinned at each other. "You know we're almost done with the whole garden," Trevor said. "Are you just adding stories until we get it all done?"

The old man laughed. "Well, that did cross my mind, but there is one last story about yet another shipment of gold, this time good American gold dollars."

"Ok, let's hear it," Andy said.

"Run those strawberries up to the house and tell your grandma we'll be in for lunch in about fifteen minutes," the old man said.

Andy ran up to the house and returned and squatted next to Trevor and looked up expectantly.

"Ok, well, you remember I told you about the counterfeiters and river pirates that worked the river? Well this has to do with them.

It seems that there was yet another shipment of gold that was being carried down the river on boats. This was money to pay the soldiers at Fort Crawford near Prairie du Chein. Again, the boats were in this area when the pirates and thieves attacked the boat and overtook it. There is a story that the boat was a huge raft that was set on fire and sank. At any rate, the gold was stolen by the pirates and supposedly they also took their loot to Bogus Bluff and hid it in the cave. There's also a story that says the bulk of the gold is still on the bottom of the river out there someplace near Bogus Bluff. That story is a little less clear than the Indian stories."

"So is any of it true?" Andy asked.

"Again, that's the million dollar question isn't it?"

"So it's all just a story?"

"I think some of it may be a little far fetched but I also think most of these old stories were based on events that happened. There were few people back then who knew how to read and write, so there were few things written down. Stories like this were passed from father to son and so on. A traveler coming through the area probably met locals and while enjoying an adult beverage at the local inn or public house, the yarn was spun and it got carried onto other places by the traveler. You know how people like to embellish stories. What might have been a bag of gold became a chest of gold and so on. Most likely every cave in the country has a treasure story attached to it. But if I had to guess, I'd say at least part of this is probably true."

"Why do you say part of it?" Trevor asked.

"Well, I have to think that the two stories about the Indians raiding the boats and hiding the treasure have a good chance of being true. The story about the river pirates makes me wonder though. For one thing, why would the pirates hide their gold up in that cave, right where the Indians hid theirs? Why not take it downriver and spend it someplace? It makes little sense to me that three different treasures were hidden in the same cave."

"So you think the last one is just a story?"

The old man shrugged. "Boys, I have no idea. It just seems strange to me that three similar stories all end up with gold being hidden in Bogus Bluff. If I had to guess, I'd say one or both of the Indian stories transformed over the years into the river pirate story. But you never know."

"No one ever has found any though?"

"Again, no one knows. If someone found it, they kept it quiet and spent it a little at a time. Heaven knows there have been many people hunting for it over the years."

"A lot of people looked for it?" Andy asked.

"There has been everything from Cornish miners from Mineral Point and New Diggings who dug dozens of holes looking for the sealed tunnels to a psychic from Madison who had visions of the gold and directed teams of treasure hunters to where he thought it was hidden. They've even brought ground penetrating radar units out here to look for it but couldn't find a way to get them up the steep hill. It's been looked for time and time again and from what I know, it's not been found.

There was an old guy named Siefert who was quite a famous painter who lived in the area and he spent years looking for it. He claimed he did find it but no one knows for sure. It's said that on his deathbed he told his family to 'look under the big flat rock on the west side of the hill'". When they began looking they found hundreds of big flat rocks on the west side of the hill and all they found under them was a rattlesnake den or two."

"So you think it's all just a story."

"I didn't say that. I just said as far as I know nobody's ever found any gold. Is it there or not.....I don't know. I *do* know this gardening has given me a great appetite and since you seem to have run out of garden to weed, I'd suggest we go up and see what your grandmother has for lunch for us."

The boys looked at the garden and it looked like it should be on the front of Home and Garden magazine.

"Looks pretty good," Trevor said.

"Come back in a week and we'll have more stories," Gramps said cackling with laughter.

They walked up to the house and had a feast, topped off with strawberry shortcake.

Chapter 6

The boys both had to work that afternoon so they rode uptown together. Trevor parked his jeep in the parking lot and they went to their places of work, Trevor to the grocery store and Andy to the hardware store.

There was brisk business in the hardware store and the time passed quickly. Andy was the first one off work as his store closed at 8 pm. He walked across the parking lot and sat in the passenger seat of the jeep and kind of dozed off. An hour later he woke as Trevor opened the driver's door.

"Napping?" he asked.

Andy grinned. "I'm plumb tuckered out after all that weed pulling this morning and we had a real busy day selling nuts and bolts and stuff."

Trevor laughed. "That Gramps, he thought he was pulling a fast one on us, but he didn't know we'd planned on weeding the garden all the while."

"We'll just let him think he outfoxed us," Andy said.

"Oh by the way.....I called Gramps when I was on my break and asked him if he knew who owned the land where Bogus Bluff is and he said he did. He called me just before I was finished working and said he'd called the guy and it was ok for us to explore it if we wanted. He said the guy was happy to let us and was glad we took time to ask instead of just going on his land without asking. I guess he's worried some dope will go up there and get hurt or killed and then he'll get sued. Gramps stood up for us and said we were ok, so if we want to go and explore it, we're good."

"Cool, I was thinking about it all the while I was working," Trevor said. "I know the gold stories are probably all just stories and even if they were true, that was nearly two hundred years ago. I'm sure if there ever was any gold, someone already found it. But I think it'd be fun to go and look the place over, don't you?"

Andy nodded and began to smile. He reached over the seat and pulled a package up in front. He opened the package and took two headlamps out of the bag.

"These are LED headlamps. They're for campers and people who work in dark places, like a plumber or something. You just put them over your head with this elastic band and then when you go in the dark you turn them on." He placed the device on his head and flipped a little switch. The tiny LED in the lamp lit up with a very bright light.

"Ho, that's great. I didn't think it'd be so bright," Trevor said.

"They're the newest thing," Andy said. "They make stoplights from them and lots of other lights too. This past Christmas we sold Christmas lights that were LED. They use almost no energy and last forever. These should stay working for 24 hours or more on just one battery."

"Wow, that's good. I was thinking of getting way back in that cave and having our flashlight go out. That'd be kind of scary."

"We won't have to worry about that with these," Andy said. "Plus with them on our head we'll have our hands free to carry gold coins back."

"Oh yeah, that's a good idea," Trevor said giggling, "Let's go out there and look at it,"

"What now?"

"Sure, I don't mean go up there, let's just drive out there and take a look at it. There's a pretty good moon, we should be able to see pretty well. After all of that treasure talk I'm kind of hyped up. I don't think I could go to sleep right now anyway."

Andy grinned. "Ok, what the heck? We've got nothing better to do."

They stopped at the gas station and got a couple of large sodas and headed out across the bridge and up the north side of the river. When they got to the area they thought was near Bogus Bluff they slowed down and watched up the hillsides for the cave.

"I think that's the sandbar we were fishing on," Andy said pointing out to the river.

In the moonlight they could see a sandbar next to the south bank of the river.

"Yeah that's it," Trevor said. "There is the treetop where you got that big smallmouth." He looked out his window and then slowed way down. "I think this is it."

He pulled off the road and parked the jeep and the boys got out. They let their eyes adjust to the darkness and soon they could make out the cave entrance up on the hill.

"Holy smokes, that's a long way up there," Andy said.

"Gramps said it was 200 feet above the river, that's 2/3 of a football field."

"It's steep," Andy said looking up at the sheer rock wall.

"No kidding. I think I see a Bighorn Sheep sleeping on that ledge up there."

Both of them burst out laughing.

"Don't laugh, we're gonna need to be like sheep to get up there," Trevor said.

"There has to be some kind of trail. People have been going up and down here for a long time. We probably can't see it in the dark but there has to be a trail."

"Yeah you're right. What do you think? I don't have to work until 1 pm again tomorrow.....how about you?"

"Me too......same as today.....I go in at 1 just like you do."

"Well, why don't you spend the night at my house and we'll get up early, have some breakfast and do a little hiking up the hill?" Andy suggested.

"Sounds like a plan to me," Trevor said.

They got into the jeep and went down the road a little way and found a place where they could turn around. As they drove back past Bogus Bluff Andy said, "Just think though, if......if there still is some gold up there. That'd be really cool."

"We won't count our Doubloons before they're found though," Trevor answered.

"Spoil sport!"

"I just hope we don't encounter a rattlesnake in that cave. As scared of snakes as you are, I'd probably have to haul your lifeless body out by myself," Trevor joked.

"Jeez, don't say things like that......oh man, now that's all I'll think about."

Trevor was laughing like crazy as they drove through the darkness toward home.

Chapter 7

They stopped at Trevor's house and he got some clothes and his toothbrush and off they went to Andy's house. They watched a little television and then went to bed. Andy slept in the bottom bunk of the bunk beds in his room and Trevor climbed up to the top bunk.

Andy turned out the light and lay awake thinking about their adventure in the morning. "Hey Trev, you asleep yet?" he asked quietly.

"Nope......I'm laying here thinking about tomorrow and that cave."

Andy laughed. "Me too.....but let's keep it that we're going exploring, not treasure hunting. That way we won't come home disappointed."

"Yeah, you're right. The chances of treasure actually being there in the first place are pretty slim and the chance that someone else hasn't found it is even less. But I guess we can always hope."

"Well, I'm not going to pick out a new sports car just yet."

Trevor laughed. "That's probably a good idea. Goodnight Andy."

"Night."

The next morning Trevor woke to the smell of bacon. He hung his head over the side of the bed and saw Andy's bed was empty. He got up and pulled on his shorts and walked to the kitchen where Andy was just taking bacon from a frying pan and putting it on a plate lined with paper towels. Andy was barefoot and in his shorts just as Trevor was.

"Better be careful, that bacon will pop and get hot grease on your belly," Trevor said yawning.

"Its just about ready......I'm going to scramble some eggs. The toast just popped up. Will you get it and butter it?"

Trevor retrieved the toast and asked, "Where's your mom?"

"She had to go in to work early. She left an hour ago."

Andy dished up the eggs and the boys sat and ate the big breakfast. When all the food was gone Trevor pushed his chair back and patted his flat belly.

"Jeez if I ate like that every day I'd have to work for weeks to get down to my wrestling weight."

Andy shook his head. "That's why I play football. You don't have to diet to do that."

They showered and dressed in shorts, tee shirts and tennis shoes. They grabbed a couple of bottles of water and their headlamps and headed to the jeep. It was a beautiful morning with a sunny sky and a nice breeze making the river look like corduroy with the little rows of waves. They parked below Bogus Bluff and got out.

"Gramps said there's a trail from the east side of the bottom of the hill," Andy said.

They hiked down the road a little way and crossed the fence and found the trail. It was like a deer trail, about a foot wide and covered with tracks of animals.

"Looks like this is the trail," Trevor said.

"Gramps also said to be careful. There are rattlesnakes in these hills. He said that they like these rocky places for dens. He said to be cautious when we're around flat rocks with dark places under them and to be sure where we put our hands when we're climbing."

"Do you think he was trying to scare us?"

"No I don't think so. I remember a neighbor I used to have when I was a kid and he used to go rattlesnake hunting in the hills. He had a stick with a big hook on the end and would dig back under flat rocks in places like this to find them. He used to call me over to see the snakes he caught."

"What did he do with them?"

37

"I think he got a bounty for them. I don't remember very well. I was probably only 5 or 6. He'd bring them back in a 5 gallon bucket. I about pooped the first time he took off the lid and I looked over the top to see those big snakes all coiled up in there. When he took the lid off they'd start rattling. Yikes, it was really scary. Once he talked me into going with him. We climbed up on a hillside just like this only not so steep. I was scared to death. All I did was find a spot where I could see for about ten feet around me that there were no snakes and I stood there like a statue while he hunted. Thankfully he didn't find any that day."

Trevor laughed. "Your one and only time snake hunting?"

"You got that right. Snakes and me don't mix. Every time he'd put that stick back under a slab of rock, I'd pray that there was no snake there."

"Well in that case, I'll go first."

Andy stood back and smiled as Trevor passed him.

"After you," he said.

The trail was pretty easy walking. It started up across the front of the hill and rose gradually up towards the steeper, rockier area. There was grass and brush along the trail so Trevor picked up a stick and tapped at places he was unsure of just in case something slithery was lurking there.

They hiked for several minutes and were probably 50 or 60 feet above the road when the trail started back along the side of the hill to the ridge.

"Looks like our trail goes the wrong way," Trevor said.

Andy looked up the hill. "There's kind of a trail up toward that ledge up there," he said pointing.

"Yeah, I see it, well, here goes nothing," Trevor said carefully finding a safe step.

The hill was covered with piles of loose shale and rocks that had fallen from higher up. There were bare places that were just smooth sandstone also. The boys had to carefully find safe footing in the loose gravel and then try to keep from sliding off the bare flat stones. It was tedious and very tiring.

They were both sweating by the time they got to the lower end of a long ledge that ran across the face of the cliff. They were now at least a hundred feet above the road.

"Whew, that was kind of scary," Trevor said wiping his face on his sleeve."

"No kidding. It kind of makes me wonder about people coming up here to counterfeit. They must have had a better way up and down than this."

"Boy, you'd think so. Well what do we do now?" Trevor asked.

Andy looked up. "It looks like we have to get up on that ledge. It goes up pretty gradually to another ledge. I don't see any other way up there. It looks like these trails zigzag back and forth across the face of this hill."

Trevor nodded. "Well I guess I'm lighter. You want to boost me up?"

Andy nodded. "Take a peek over the top before you grab anything up there. It'd be bad to grab a rattler without looking first. Or look up there and get nailed between the eyes." He made a step with his hands and Trevor put his foot into it. Then he lifted and Trevor grasped the edge of the ledge. He carefully looked up onto the ledge and seemed satisfied it was safe. He gripped the edge and pulled himself up onto the ledge. Andy lifted as Trevor pulled himself up and over.

Andy waited. "Trev?"

Suddenly Trevor's face appeared over the ledge. "This is cool. It's a lot less steep than where we just came from. He put his hands down and Andy took them in his hands and Trevor pulled him up far enough that he could grab the ledge himself and he climbed over the edge.

The ledge was about three feet wide and went up gradually across the cliff face another 30 or 40 feet. There was a mirror ledge at the other end that went up the last distance to the cave entrance.

"Well, let's go," Trevor said walking up the ledge.

They got to the other end and Andy boosted Trevor up the last leg of their journey.

"This one's a lot narrower," Trevor said when he lay down to help Andy up.

When they were both up on the ledge Andy saw what Trevor meant. This one was only a foot to maybe fifteen inches wide and had a lot of fine gravel and sand on it.

"We better be careful on this one. It's a long way to the bottom from here," he said.

"It's not the drop, it's that sudden stop at the bottom that worries me," Trevor said.

Andy smacked him in the shoulder.

They crossed carefully over the last ledge and then climbed up over one last cliff face and they were there.

"Holy smokes it's a lot bigger than I expected," Andy said looking at the hole in the face of the hill.

"It's the size of a double door in a house almost," Trevor said. He inspected the door closely. "It's been enlarged," he said. "You can see here where somebody chiseled it to make it taller. I suppose they got tired of crawling in on their hands and knees."

They looked back into the dark cave and turned to one another.

"Well, here we are," Andy said.

"That we are," Trevor added.

Chapter 8

T revor went in first. The entrance to the cave was dry and scattered with leaves and small rocks and sand. The deeper they went into the cave the darker it got so they put the elastic bands around their heads and switched on their head lamps.

The entrance was pretty wide open and they soon saw three tunnels leading deeper into the cave.

"Gramps said the left and right ones went a long way into the hill," Trevor said.

"Yeah, this middle one supposedly goes to a room. I think we should check that one out first don't you?" Andy replied.

Trevor nodded. They started down the middle tunnel. After ten feet or so the tunnel narrowed down on the sides and the ceiling got lower and they had to stoop over to walk. Soon they had to get on their hands and knees.

"Getting kind of spooky," Andy said. His voice echoed in the tight rocky space.

They crawled through a small hole and were surprised when they emerged in a small room.

"Wow, this is just like Gramps said," Andy exclaimed.

The room was about the size of a small bedroom or a big bathroom. The walls and ceiling had obviously been carved with chisels and tools. There were marks where rock had been broken away to enlarge the room. Up on the sides there were nooks created as if they were to store food or clothing to keep it up off the floor. At the back end, the room narrowed down to a tunnel again.

"Look at the ceiling," Trevor said. "It's all black, like there was fire in here or maybe candles."

"Probably candles or oil lanterns," Andy said. "They couldn't have a fire or it'd get real smoky."

The walls had graffiti scrawled all over their faces. Some of the graffiti was carved as if with a chisel and hammer and some was painted on or written with marker.

"Look here," Trevor said pointing to a carving. 'GT and RW were here July 9, 1906'."

"Here's one, 'Cal and Laura True Love'".

"Oh man, what a place to take a date," Trevor laughed.

They looked at all of the scratching and more recent magic marker graffiti and realized there had been dozens if not scores of people here ahead of them.

The floor was littered with old food cans that had been opened and discarded back against the tunnel in the back. There were also more recent beer cans and soda cans as well as a few pieces of clothing like a sock and an old hat.

"God only knows what must have gone on in here," Andy said.

"I don't think I want to know," Trevor said, especially old Cal and Laura."

They looked in the nooks and found more old cans and an old jackknife that was all rusted. Trevor got down on his hands and knees and pulled away some of the junk from the back tunnel. He stuck his head into the opening. "Only goes a few feet to a solid wall," he said.

Then he shouted, "Holy smokes, Andy, a coin!"

Trevor came scooting back out of the hole with a large coin in his hand. It was covered with mud and dirt. He spit on it and rubbed his thumb across it.

"It's not gold, it looks like silver," Andy said.

Trevor cleared the coin off and then looked up and grinned.

"It's a half dollar. The date on it is 1953."

They laughed. Trevor handed the coin to Andy.

"Well actually this isn't just some 50 cent piece," he said. "This is from when they made coins from real silver, not like the ones we have now that are silver over some kind of other metal in the middle. This is probably worth a few bucks."

Trevor grinned. "Well, we're a few bucks closer to being millionaires then aren't we?"

They scratched around in the sand and dirt and debris looking for any more old coins but didn't find any. They did run across an old metal button that looked like it had been from long ago. Andy got excited when he saw what he thought was another coin but it turned out to be an old Nehi soda bottle cap.

"Well, so much for this room."

Trevor opened his phone and looked at the time.

"It's almost noon already," he said. "We don't have time to go down any more tunnels. We better start back or we'll be late for work."

They crawled back out of the room and then back into the sunlight. They had to shield their eyes for a minute until they got used to the light. Andy began to laugh when he looked at Trevor's face all smeared with dirt from rummaging around in the cave. His hands and knees were black with mud.

"You're not so clean yourself," Trevor said looking over his friend. "I guess the plan from now on is to wear old clothes and not worry about trying to keep clean."

They started back down the long trail to the bottom. It was much easier getting back down than it had been going up. They were on the last part of the lower trail when Andy stopped short and began backing up. Trevor was behind him and Andy ran into him in his haste.

"Snake!" Andy said.

"Where?"

Andy pointed to the grass on the lower side of the trail. Trevor picked up a stick and poked into the grass. Suddenly a grass snake slithered down between two big rocks and disappeared into the brush.

"A grass snake," he said grinning.

"A snake is a snake," Andy said. "You go first."

DAN BOMKAMP

Trevor grinned and took the lead and they made it back to the car unscathed.

"We're safe now," Trevor said as he shut his door."

Andy looked at his buddy. "Sometimes you can be a real pain in the butt."

They were laughing as they U turned and headed back to town.

When they got back to town Andy turned on his computer and typed "1953 half dollar" into the search engine. Several pages popped up and they chose one of them and opened it.

"Wow, that's the coin," he said looking at the picture of the Franklin Half Dollar. "Look at this, it's worth a minimum of $10 and could be worth up to $135 in excellent condition. The silver in it is worth about $5."

Trevor took the coin and compared it to the picture. "This is way nicer than that one," he said.

"It's probably not worth $135 but I bet it's worth something like $75 to $100," Andy said. "This one is pretty nice."

Trevor laughed, "Well I guess that's not too bad for a day's work, but it's a long way from a fortune in gold."

Chapter 9

T he next day the boys went to church with their moms and afterward they stopped to talk to Gramps outside the church.

"We went up to Bogus Bluff," Andy said to the old man.

"And did you put a gold coin in the collection basket today?" the old man asked with a smile on his face.

"No but we did find a coin," Trevor said producing the half dollar they'd picked up in the cave.

The old man looked it over and grinned. "Well, that's a start," he said.

"We looked it up and it could be worth between $10 and $135. We figure it's in pretty nice shape so probably somewhere in the middle," Trevor said.

The old man nodded. "Well, at least you didn't get skunked did you?"

"Gramps, do you think we're being stupid going up there? I mean I know we're probably not going to find anything but what do you think?" Andy asked.

"Well boys, the odds are this half dollar is probably more than most of the other treasure hunters have found. But, that doesn't mean that there's no treasure. I really doubt that all of those three treasures are there but it's possible that one of them is. I'd just say not to get your hopes up. Legends are usually based on some real event, so there is a chance that something might be there. If you go up there thinking you're going to be rich, you'll probably be disappointed. What you guys have to do it think 'out-of-the-box', so to speak. The Cornish miners thought that by digging cross tunnels they'd find the gold, others thought that metal detectors would find it, you have to use your heads and try to think the way the people who hid it would have thought."

"So there is a chance that there's gold up there?" Trevor asked.

The old man shrugged. "Look at it this way. You'll get plenty of exercise and become pretty good rock climbers, you'll have something to do besides exercise your thumbs on your video games and you might, just might get something in return. I guess if I was your age again, I wouldn't think it was a waste of time."

"So you looked when you were our age?"

The old man smiled. "A dozen times," he said.

"Did you carve your initials in that room in the front?" Trevor asked.

The old man grinned. "That I did."

The boys went home and changed out of their church clothes and then Trevor picked up Andy in the jeep and they headed back up the north side of the river to the cave.

"Let's take a look at the big tunnel on the west side today," Andy said as they worked their way up the three stretches of trails that crisscrossed the face of the hill. It was like going up a Z shaped trail with one stretch going west, then the trail switched back to the east and then back west again. When they got to the entrance they turned on their head lamps and walked inside.

"Let's take our time and check out anything that looks different along the tunnel," Trevor said.

"Yeah, Gramps said some people think the Indians hid the gold in a side tunnel and then sealed it up. All of those old timers who have been here were using candles and lamps that didn't give off very good light. These LED lights are really bright. We should be able to see if something looks out of the ordinary."

They started down the tunnel. For the first hundred feet it was like walking down a hallway at home and then the tunnel began to get narrower and the ceiling got lower so the boys had to crouch to walk.

They moved along slowly looking at the walls and ceiling as they walked. About two hundred feet in, they found a side tunnel that had been chiseled out of the rock.

"This must be one of the tunnels that the lead miners made," Andy said.

The tunnel was much smaller requiring the boys to crawl on their hands and knees. The floor was littered with small pieces of rock that had been created with the chisels as they hacked the tunnel out of the stone. It was hard on their knees crawling through the stuff.

"I don't like this very much" Trevor complained.

"Me either. I hope it doesn't go much farther."

They got about forty feet down the tunnel and came to the end. It had been enlarged a little bit at the end so they could turn around to crawl back out. When they got back to the main tunnel they sat down and rubbed their knees.

"Well that was a waste of time and energy," Trevor said.

"Maybe we can just bypass the rest of those. Unless we see something about one that makes it special I think they're a waste of time," Andy said.

They continued down the main tunnel. About every hundred feet they found another side tunnel that went off the main tunnel to the east, toward the middle of the hill. They skipped the next two of them. Then they came to a side tunnel that ran off to the left, to the side of the hill.

"Let's look at this one," Trevor suggested.

They crawled into the tunnel and it was different than the other one had been. It was clear of debris.

"This one looks older, and whoever made it cleaned it up,"

Andy said.

"This looks more like the main tunnel. Maybe it's a natural one made when the others were made by rain," Trevor added.

They followed the tunnel for close to a hundred feet and soon saw light up ahead. Andy was in the lead and suddenly he stopped and began to back up.

"What're you doing?" Trevor said as Andy's rear end banged into his face.

"Back up!"

"What's wrong?

"There's a rattlesnake up ahead! Hurry back up!"

Trevor began to crawl backwards as fast as he could. Andy was right behind him and kept running into him.

"Slow down a little, your sticking your butt right in my face," Trevor said laughing.

"Hurry up!"

They got back to the main tunnel and sat down on the floor panting for breath.

"You saw a snake?" Trevor asked.

"I saw his tail, his rattle."

"Was he shaking it?"

Andy thought for a second. "Well, no it was just lying there. The tunnel turned a little and I saw the rattle sticking just past the turn. We were close to the outside. I saw some leaves and stuff on the floor too."

Trevor looked at Andy with a half grin on his face. "So you saw his rattle but no snake?"

"I saw something that looked like a rattle and I wasn't taking any chances," Andy said.

Trevor grinned. "Wait here," he said.

"What'r you gonna do?"

"I'm going to go and see that rattlesnake," Trevor replied.

Trevor crawled back down the tunnel and Andy watched his light until he got too far for him to see it any more. He sat there looking back and forth down the main tunnel with his head lamp and felt a little uncertain.

"It's a lot less spooky when you're not alone," he thought to himself.

It seemed like a long time but eventually he saw Trevor's light coming back down the side tunnel.

"So?" he said.

Trevor emerged into the main tunnel and sat down. "I found the outside. It's on the side of the hill about half way up. I also found this," he said tossing a half a corn cob into Andy's lap.

Andy jumped up and hit his head on the ceiling. "Ow!" he yelled. Then he looked down to the floor and realized what the object was. "Jeez, what a dickhead," he said rubbing the top of his head.

Trevor was laughing like crazy.

"Back up! Rattlesnake!" Trevor was mocking him laughing his head off.

Andy punched him in the arm. "Nobody likes a smart ass." He picked up the corn cob Trevor had tossed at him and threw it at Trevor hitting him in the forehead.

He began moving down the main tunnel again and left Trevor behind still laughing.

Chapter 10

The boys continued down the tunnel passing three more excavations on the right side of the main tunnel that probably had been made by the Cornish miners. They all were pretty much the same, small, cramped and full of sharp chunks of stone.

Andy got over his little mad and had to grin to himself. He felt a little silly about the snake tail thing but snakes were definitely not his friends. He'd been afraid of them for as long as he could remember.

"Just what is it with you and snakes?" Trevor asked.

"I was traumatized when I was just five years old," Andy said.

"Traumatized?" Trevor laughed. "What happened?"

"I'm not going to tell you if you're going to laugh about it."

"Sorry, please tell me." Trevor tried to look serious but was having a hard time keeping a straight face.

"Well, I was over at my friend Tommy's place and it was hot and we were playing in his sandbox in the back yard. We'd taken off our shirts and shoes and socks. I was wearing board shorts and we were playing with trucks and stuff. Tommy had one of those little blow-up swimming pools and it was nearly empty. The water in it was all dirty so we decided to lift it up and empty it and then fill it up and go swimming."

"Well, we lifted it up and there was a nest under there and there. We stood there looking at the nest of grass and leaves and suddenly it began to move around. Then baby snakes began crawling out of the nest. There were about a hundred little baby snakes in it."

"A hundred snakes?"

"Well, it was probably more like ten or twelve, but they were crawling everywhere and it looked like a heck of a bunch of them."

"Ok, so then what?"

"Well we dropped the swimming pool and the snakes started coming out from under it and crawled over our bare feet and all over the place. Of course we were screaming our heads off and started to run away."

"How big were these snakes?" Trevor asked.

"I suppose ten inches, maybe a foot long."

Trevor nodded and stifled a grin.

"So anyway I ran out in the yard and was standing there terrified, and suddenly I felt something crawling up the inside of my pants leg. I undid the button on top and in my haste I pulled not only my shorts down but also my underwear. Well sure enough there was a snake in my pants. So I began to scream and kick and my pants and underwear flew off and into the bushes. There were snakes everywhere so I began running back home.....buck naked, screaming my head off."

By now Trevor had tears running down his face from laughing so hard.

"It wasn't funny!" Andy said.

Trevor couldn't talk.

"Well, ok it probably was pretty funny but I didn't care. I lived about two blocks from Tommy's house and when I came running into the house buck naked my mom almost had a heart attack."

"So that's what caused you to be so afraid of snakes," Trevor said.

"Yup and I never wore those shorts again and never went to Tommy's to play again."

"Well, I can understand that. It must have been very... traumatizing."

Andy glared at him. "You said you wouldn't laugh."

"Do you really think I could keep from laughing at a story like that?"

Andy grinned, "I guess not but keep it to yourself. I don't want the guys on the baseball team to think I'm a sissy."

"So, do you want me to lead down this tunnel, just in case we find a swimming pool full of snakes?" Trevor asked.

"Shut up!" Andy replied.

Trevor laughed, "Just asking, jeez, touchy."

"Ok, you lead." Andy said, and off they went down the tunnel.

It seemed that they were rising as they moved along.

"My back's getting tired of this bent over walking," Andy said.

"Me too.....it can't be too far to the end. We've gone a long way already."

Trevor had no more than said that when he stopped and turned to Andy.

"I see light," he said.

They moved ahead and soon came to an opening in the side of the hill near the top of the ridge. The sun was really bright and they had to shield their eyes at first. They switched off their head lamps and looked around.

They were in a swale where two ridges came together creating a low spot. There was brush and a treetop lying in the swale.

"This must be where the tunnel started," Andy said. "Remember Gramps said these caves were made by rainwater collecting in a sink hole? This must be where the sinkhole was."

Trevor nodded. "That makes sense. Then as it got bigger and bigger the rainwater ran down this ditch and made the cave bigger and bigger over the years. It must have taken thousands of years to erode it out like it is."

Andy nodded. "Kind of makes 60 or 70 years of a human lifetime kind of insignificant doesn't it?"

They climbed up out of the swale and stood there looking around trying to figure out where they were compared to where they'd started.

"So I'll bet you that side tunnel where the "snake tail" was is where the counterfeiters got out and made their getaway."

"That makes sense," Trevor said.

"That's got to be the next hill to the west," Andy said pointing across to the other hillside. Let's climb up to the top and walk this ridge back toward the river."

They did just that. The hill was steep and it took some doing to get to the top. Once on top the hill flattened out and was fairly open. They followed a game trail towards the south end of the ridge.

Suddenly they came up over a little rise and there was the river below them. The sun was shining and the wind was stirring up the water making the surface look like diamonds flashing in the bright light. The sandbars looked like tan patches on a blue quilt.

"Wow, what a view," Trevor exclaimed.

"No kidding, you can see for miles."

They walked to the east side of the bluff and could see the river for many miles coming from the east.

"I had no idea it curved back and forth so much," Andy said as he noticed the zigzagging of the water, back and forth down the valley.

"Me either. It looks like one of those trout streams you see up in the hills that meander back and forth up a valley."

"I don't want to sound like I'm some kind of know-it-all, but do you know why those streams and the river meander like that?"

Trevor grinned. "I have a feeling I'm going to learn."

"I was watching one of those National Geographic shows once and they talked about it. The current flows down the stream but instead of just flowing straight and flat it flows like a corkscrew. The spinning of the earth causes the water to move around like it does when you flush the toilet. That corkscrewing current eats away the bank in places where it's softer than others and soon it makes a loop. Over the centuries the loop moves farther and farther out and soon the river has a bend in it. Sometimes the bend gets so far out it actually gets cut off when there's a flood. Then that part is left behind. They call that an oxbow. It's a little C shaped pond that once was part of the stream."

Trevor nodded. "Thank you professor.....that was very clear."

"Oh shut up."

Trevor was cackling as he edged near the front of the bluff. "It's pretty steep but I think we can shinny down over this front and get to the ledge where the cave opening is."

"That sounds good to me. I sure don't want to go all the way back and crouch all the way back through that tunnel."

Trevor started out with Andy close behind. The hill was very steep but there were trees and bushes to hang onto that let them work their way down. Andy was very careful about where he put his hands when he was grabbing for a hold. The 'snake tail' in the cave was as close as he wanted to get to any snake today. Soon they saw the ledge below them and worked their way to the west side of it. They had to slide down a large flat rock to the ledge.

Once they were safely on the ledge they brushed themselves off. "Well two tunnels explored. Not much to show for it though," Trevor said.

"Well we do have half a dollar," Andy joked.

"That we do. Well I've had enough darkness for one day.....how about you?"

Andy nodded. "I say we get the boat and go fishing for the rest of the day."

And that is what they did.

Chapter 11

B oth of the boys had to work the next day so the treasure hunt was postponed. Andy was in the automotive aisle stocking shelves when he noticed someone coming toward him. He turned and smiled when he saw his grandpa approaching.

"So, still working? I thought you guys would be out buying new Porches today."

"No we're going to wait on that," Andy said. "What's up?"

"Oh I need a quart of oil for the lawn mower so I thought I'd stop and say hi," the old man said.

"Are you going to mow the grass?"

"Of course," the old man said. "I take it in little sections. I mow for ten or fifteen minutes and then take a rest. It takes most of the day but I have nothing else to do. If I get real tired I can just lay down on the lawn and rest."

Andy knew he was getting conned. "Why don't you get your little mower ready and then Trev and I will come over after work. We'll bring our riding mower and I can ride and Trev can trim with yours. We'll have it done in half an hour."

"Oh that's ok, if I take it easy I won't have to worry about a heart attack or anything," the old man said stifling a grin. "Of course if I did drop dead in the middle of the lawn it'd sure ruin the day for your grandma."

"I've got an idea," Andy said. "We'll cut the grass and you make burgers on the grill."

"Deal," his granddad said.

Andy watched his grandpa walk down the aisle and smiled. The old man had been there for him any time he'd needed him. When his parents split up it would have been much harder if he'd not had Gramps to turn to.

He got off work at 5 and walked across the parking lot to the grocery store. Trevor was bagging groceries.

"What time are you off?" Andy asked.

"Ten minutes ago....but we got busy. I'll be done when this little rush is over. What are we going to do?"

"Gramps came in and I volunteered us to mow his grass. We'll take our rider over and one can ride and the other trim. He'll feed us afterward."

"Sounds good to me.....maybe we can get some more of his Bogus Bluff knowledge out of him while we're there."

An hour later they were just finishing up the grass. Andy drove the riding mower over by the driveway and parked it. Trevor put the push mower into the garage and they went into the house and washed up.

"I'll start the burgers," Gramps said.

The boys carried all of the other goodies his grandma had fixed out to the patio and they sat and chatted with Andy's grandparents while they waited for the burgers. When they were finished they sat down to eat.

"So you've been up to the caves?" his grandma asked.

"Yeah, we went through two of them. We still have the east one to look at."

"Oh that's the narrow one," the old lady said.

"You've been up there?" Andy asked.

"Years ago.....we went up there when we were teenagers didn't we Henry?" she said.

His grandpa grinned. "Yes we did," he said wiggling his eyebrows.

"Ewww!" Andy said. "Don't tell me anymore. That's gross."

The old folks laughed. "What.....don't you guys think we were young and in love once?"

56

"It's just not something I like to think about."

Grandma cackled. "That narrow tunnel comes out over by Judith's Point."

"Judith's what?"

"The next hill to the east has a narrow hilltop that ends in a sheer cliff. The story goes that there was a young maiden named Judith McCloud who was out picking berries on the hill when a band of Indians came along and tried to take her captive. Rather than be taken by savages she ran for her life and when she came to the end of the hill, she plunged over the cliff to her death."

"So this fair maiden was out minding her own business picking berries and along came a band of savages?" Andy asked.

"It would seem that the local savages just happened by," his grandma said. "And Judith being a Godly woman felt it was more appropriate to fling herself off the cliff than be ravaged by a savage."

The boy burst out laughing. "Granny, listen to you!" Andy said.

"You forgot that little tidbit?" Trevor said to Gramps.

"I didn't think it pertained to the hidden treasure," the old man said. "No more than the Indian burial cave that is supposedly up there someplace."

"Another treasure you overlooked? Andy asked.

"Well again, this is probably just a story, but supposedly someplace up there there's a huge flat stone that hides the entrance to an Indian burial chamber. There are stories of men who found it and lowered themselves down to a chamber fifty feet under the surface. From there they left one man on a ledge and he lowered the rest down another fifty feet into another chamber and then they did that same thing again to yet another chamber. This lowest chamber was filled with gold and precious gems and there were shelves built that housed hundreds of skeletons. The story was that it was the burial place of chiefs for many generations."

"And that just slipped your mind?" Andy asked.

"I'm old I forget," the old man grinned.

"Are you sure you didn't see that in some movie about pharos?" Andy asked.

"I'm just answering your question about the burial treasure. I have no opinion as to its truthfulness or falsehood."

"So what you're saying is that we've got lots more looking to do," Trevor said.

"Boys, as I've said before, as long as you're careful I think you'll have a great adventure up there. But I wouldn't be putting a down payment on any new toys just yet. I'm not saying all of these stories are lies, and I'm not saying they're true. You guys are clever. If there is something to find, I'd put my money on you two to figure it out."

"Thanks Gramps. If we do find a treasure, we'll share it with you and Grandma. You can take a cruise to the Bahamas."

"Oooh, I'm going in the house right now and order a thong," the old man said.

Grandma wiggled her eyebrows at her husband and Andy and Trevor said, "Ewww."

Chapter 12

S ince both Andy and Trevor had afternoon shifts again the next day they decided to go and take a look at the east tunnel. Andy stayed over at Trevor's and they got up early so they'd have plenty of time to explore. After they had breakfast they drove up the north side of the river and parked in their usual spot. When they got out Trevor looked to the east and said, "That must be Judith's Point."

Andy looked and nodded. "Jeez that'd be a pretty nasty drop. It looks like a good hundred feet until you'd hit something."

"Do you think that story is real?" Trevor asked.

Andy shrugged. "I suppose it's possible. Have you ever heard of a little town over on the Mississippi called Maiden Rock? It's just a wide spot in the road with a gas station and a few houses north of La Crosse. It's named after a young girl who was being chased by Indians who wanted to take her captive and she ran to the end of the hill and jumped to her death rather than be savaged by the savages. Sound familiar?"

Trevor grinned. "I'd bet there are some type of point or rock cliffs all over the country with the same story. Just like there's a treasure linked to every cave in the country."

"Yeah, I think so too. A high point with a sharp drop is a perfect setting for a maiden story and a cave that is dark and spooky is perfect for a hidden treasure story."

"Well, shall we hike up and look at that last tunnel?"

Trevor nodded. "We shall."

They hiked over to the hill and began the switchbacks that led up to the cave. It took less time every time they did it because they were more used to the trail and weren't as cautious as they had been the first time they climbed it. When they got to the top they stopped for a breather.

"Well, if this one is as narrow as they say it is, we'll probably have to go all the way to the end. We won't be able to turn around," Andy said.

Trevor nodded. "I was thinking that. Still want to go?"

Andy didn't answer, but walked into the door of the cave and turned on his light. Trevor followed him and they started down the tunnel.

At first they could stoop and walk but soon the tunnel narrowed down too much for walking and they had to crawl on their hands and knees.

"It's a good thing the floor is covered with mud or our knees would be all sore by the time we get out of here," Trevor said. His voice sounded strange as his echoed down the tunnel.

"Yeah, I suppose it's moist in here all the time. It's pretty cool too."

"Why don't you say it?" Trevor asked.

"What? What should I say?"

"It's probably too cool in here for snakes."

"Shut up. Jeez, I wasn't even thinking about snakes and now....well now I am."

Trevor chuckled. "Too bad you went first."

"Lucky for you we can't pass each other."

On they went. They crawled for what seemed like several hundred feet. It was hard to tell in the narrow tunnel. After a quarter of an hour of crawling the tunnel began to narrow down even more.

"We're going to have to belly crawl," Andy said.

"I'm right behind you," Trevor replied. "Just don't stop quickly or I'll be eating a shoe."

The pace was slower now. They had to use their elbows and toes to scoot forward to make any progress. The walls and ceiling seemed to get even narrower as they moved on.

"It's a good thing we're not big football players," Trevor said. "We'd never be able to get through here."

"I'm a football player," Andy said.

"Well, I mean a lineman, you're one of those skinny little backs and they're pretty petite."

Andy didn't say anything. He'd been having a little gas pain now and then and he decided to rid himself of the pressure. He concentrated and let a blast go. It echoed down the tunnel like the sound of a hotrod motorcycle revving its motor.

"Holy smokes!" Trevor gasped. "That just about scared me to death. Oh my gosh, oh what the heck have you been eating?"

Andy was laughing so hard he couldn't answer.

"Move ahead, hurry up, man...it stinks back here!" Trevor said excitedly.

"Just remember that the next time you make disparaging comments about my football abilities," Andy chuckled.

Trevor laughed. "Disparaging.....jeez you learned a new word."

"Oh shut up," Andy said.

They slid on and on for many minutes. The tunnel was mostly smooth on the sides and there were no marks where anyone had tried to cut a side tunnel.

"Nobody's been in here making any extra passages," Trevor said.

"I can see why. Imagine trying to hammer in this narrow of a space?"

On they went. The tunnel seemed to be pretty straight and level. After nearly half an hour of sliding in the mud they began to feel warmth.

"The end must be ahead, feel that breeze? Andy asked.

"Yeah, and it smells a lot better up here too."

Soon they could see light up ahead. In a few minutes they emerged from the ground and found themselves on the east side of the hill, half way up the side of a ditch that had been formed between Bogus Bluff and Judith's hill.

"We're in a sinkhole again," Andy said.

"It's not really a sinkhole.....it's more like a ditch."

"Well, I'm sure a long time ago it was a low spot between these two hills and with rain and erosion it turned into a sinkhole."

Trevor nodded in agreement. "So what Gramps said about how the cave was formed was right. Acid rain gathered in the sinkhole and eventually dissolved the limestone vein that ran through the hill. Then as the space got bigger and bigger it turned into a cave and more and more rain ran into it, and made it larger and larger."

"Do you suppose water still runs down it sometimes? I mean when it really rains. It looks like all of the water from these two hillsides ends up in this ditch. I'll bet when we get a big thunderstorm this fills up and the excess runs right down that tunnel."

Trevor nodded. "That's why the floor is covered with mud. Remind me not to go exploring in there when a storm is on the horizon."

They stood there looking around trying to decide which way to go back. They had three choices. One was to go back through the cave. Choice two was to climb down the steep hillside and go through the brush to the road and three was to climb up to the pretty much open hilltop and go back down over the front like they did when they came out of the west tunnel.

"Back through the cave is definitely out," Trevor said.

"I'm not in a big hurry to crawl through all the brush and...ok I'll say it.....snake territory," Andy added.

"Well back up the hill then," Trevor said.

They hiked back up and then walked to the front of the hill. They stood there looking out over miles of river valley.

"If nothing else, this view is pretty spectacular," Andy said.

"Well you're right about that. And don't forget we did find half a dollar."

They were giggling and laughing as they shinnied down to the top ledge. Then they climbed down to the bottom and headed home. They were a little disappointed but they'd kept their expectations low, so the adventure had still been worth the effort.

Their clothes were muddy and their knees and elbows were a little raw but it had been a pretty good time exploring the dark passages.

Chapter 13

When the boys got back to town they realized how covered they were with mud from shinnying up the tunnel so they went to the river, took off their shoes and jumped in, clothes and all. They scrubbed themselves clean and then took off their shirts and shorts and scrubbed the mud out of them. They put their shorts back on and drove home for a real shower.

That afternoon they both had to work and after work that night they were both pretty tired out so they went to their own homes and got a good night's sleep.

The next morning they went to see Gramps. He was interested in their story of the tunnel and their theory that the tunnels had been made as he had told them from sinkholes that gathered the water over the centuries and created the holes in the earth.

"Well, you learned a bit about geology and cave formation then didn't you?" the old man asked.

The boys agreed they surely had.

"So what's next?" Gramps asked.

"We're thinking of going fishing tonight and staying on a sandbar. I've got that little pup tent and if we have some luck catching a few fish, we'll have a fish fry for supper. If not, we'll take a few hotdogs along just in case."

Grandpa thought that was a good idea and he bid them farewell and retired to his recliner in the living room.

The boys got their gear together and hooked Andy's pickup onto the boat and headed to the river. They put all their gear in the boat and then Andy backed the trailer down to the water. Trevor pushed the boat off the trailer and led it back to the landing with a rope while Andy parked the truck.

They loaded up and headed upriver. On the way they stopped at several good looking spots and cast a few times to log piles and tree tops. They caught several smallmouth bass and one white bass. They turned them all back though since they didn't much care for a bass as an eating fish.

"They remind me of when I go over my boots when I'm duck hunting," Andy said once, "they taste like my socks smell with that swamp mud soaked into them."

Trevor had to agree. They were looking for a couple of walleyes or some bluegills for supper.

After a couple of hours of fishing and moving up river they arrived at the sandbar where they'd caught the big bass the day they noticed the cave on Bogus Bluff. Andy looked up at the hill and smiled.

"We won't have to wonder about it any more. We've been through the whole thing now."

"Except the part where the gold is hidden," Trevor said.

"Except that part," Andy chuckled.

They pulled the boat up on the sandbar and started fishing. Of course at first they had to try for smallmouth bass just because they were so fun to catch. They managed to get four of them out of the treetops before the bass action slowed to nothing.

Then they got a can of worms out and baited up and began fishing on the bottom below the sandbar in the deep water of the drop off. In no time Andy caught a nice walleye. He put it on the stringer and before he had it tied to the boat Trevor had a twin to it.

"One more and we've got supper," Andy said.

They fished for a short while and got not only another walleye but three nice bluegills. "That's plenty for today," Trevor said. "How about we take a swim before supper?"

They stripped off their clothes and swam in their boxers. After half an hour of fun in the water they got out and dried themselves off. They took off their boxers and hung them over the side of the boat to dry and put on their shorts, going commando.

Andy worked on setting up the tent while Trevor waded across the shallows to the island and came back with an armful of fire wood.

They had the camp ready for the evening so they lay back against a log that had been lying on the sandbar for a long time and soaked up the sun.

Andy kept looking up on the hill at Bogus Bluff. "We missed something up there Trev," he said.

"What'da ya mean?"

"I don't know for sure. There's something sticking in my brain that says we overlooked something that's a clue to the treasure."

Trevor grinned. "Do you really think it's there?"

Andy shrugged. "Maybe not all of the treasures, but one or maybe two of them, yeah, I think something is up there. Something started all of those stories. Some person a couple of hundred years ago didn't just dream up a treasure story and begin telling it. At least I don't think that's how it happened."

They sat quietly for a long while, just the sound of the river gurgling now and then or the sound of a bird in the woods calling.

"Just think.....this is probably about where the Indians attacked the boats if they really existed. Somebody could have died right here where we're sitting."

"Oh that's a cheery thought," Trevor said. "I hope I don't start thinking about that tonight when I'm trying to get to sleep."

Suddenly Andy sat up.

"How good did you look at that back end of the first tunnel.....the one where the room had been carved out?"

"I didn't look at it much at all. I kinda bent down there and it was full of trash so I just ignored it....why?"

"Ok, puzzle me this......the other two tunnels end at the face of the cliff and come from the upper part of the hill. Why does

66

that tunnel begin and end right at the cliff? How did it get created?"

"Maybe it was carved from the lower end by whoever made the room," Trevor offered.

"Ok, then if they carved it to make the room why did they keep on going a few feet farther?"

"I don't know. Maybe they got tired of carving."

"But the tunnel into the room is exactly like the other tunnels. It's shaped the same way and has the same kinds of walls. They're not chipped walls, but smooth and flat like the other caves."

Trevor thought for a minute. "I never thought of that," he said. "It must have started up the hill someplace too.......and it's blocked!"

"Gramps said the Indians sealed off the tunnel that they hid the treasure in.....at least that's how the story goes."

"Yeah, so how does that help us?"

Andy smiled to himself. "We've got to go back up there. We need to look at the back end of that room. We need to see if it just ends there or if someone blocked it to.....hide something."

"Holy crap! We might have stumbled onto something here."

'When are we going?"

Andy looked at the sun and it was only a short way from dropping over the horizon to the west. "It's too late now. Let's go first thing in the morning?"

"What about our headlamps?" Trevor asked.

Andy got up and opened the little compartment in the boat where he stored extra junk that he might need. He reached in and brought out their headlamps.

"I thought these would come in handy for night fishing sometime," he said with a wide grin. "I stuck them in here since I thought we probably were done cave exploring."

"Handy they will be.....very handy," Trevor said.

Chapter 14

A ndy had a hard time getting to sleep. Every time he'd just about doze off the cave would pop into his head and he'd think about the possibility of them really finding something of value up there. He knew the odds were not in their favor. Hundreds of people over a period of nearly 200 years had looked for the "treasure" and found nothing, so the chances were pretty good that they'd do the same. But he had a nagging thought deep in his brain that they'd stumbled onto a clue that others might have missed.

Trevor slept like a rock. Andy was jealous of his buddy for being able to sleep so easily while it eluded him. Finally he got out of his sleeping bag and crawled out of the tent.

It was cool out so he put on his shirt and walked over and stirred the embers in the fire. After adding a couple of logs, the fire flared up and lit the night. He sat there with his bare feet close to the fire warming them up. In his mind's eye he could see the Indians attacking from the shore as the boats came down the river. He could see arrows flashing across the water and hitting the boatmen. Then as the boats drifted unguided the Indians swam to them and steered them to the bank where they grabbed up the sacks of coins and worked their way up the hill.

He was playing it in his mind when Trevor shook his shoulder.

"What are you doing out here? It's freezing out."

"What? Oh, couldn't sleep, came out here, guess I fell asleep."

"Dreaming of gold I bet."

Andy grinned. "Let's go back into the tent it must be the middle of the night yet."

The next thing Andy knew he heard a frying pan clink on the cooking grate. He pulled on his shirt and shorts and crawled out to see Trevor just finishing up some scrambled eggs.

"Just in time," he said handing Andy a plate of eggs and bacon.

"You ready to go up there again?" Andy asked.

"You'd have to hogtie me to keep me back. We're gonna have to be a little careful hiking up there though. All we have is flip flops."

"We'll just take it slow and easy."

They broke camp and cleaned up everything so the sandbar looked exactly as it did before they got there. Then they motored across the river and pulled the boat up on the shore and tied it to a tree. They climbed up the river bank and crossed the road, climbed the fence and followed their path to the hill.

When they got going up the ledges they found it was easier to climb barefoot instead of wearing the flip flops, so they left them half way up the first leg of the journey.

They got up to the cave entrance, put their headlamps on and went into the cave. Andy led the way into the middle tunnel and they emerged into the room that had been the counterfeiter's lair.

The tunnel at the back of the room was exactly the same dimension of the one that led into the room from the outside. They both got down on their hands and knees and began digging junk out of the hole.

There were soda cans, a few beer cans, an old newspaper, food cans and a condom wrapper.

"Eww," Trevor said when he saw the wrapper.

"I could think of more romantic places to take a girl than this old damp cave," Andy said.

"No kidding. What a Casanova to bring a girl here."

Deep in the hole was a pair of work boots. They were worn and cracked and had leather laces.

"These look like Civil War era," Andy said.

"Maybe they're left over from the counterfeiters."

They finally got the hole cleared out. They both stuck their heads and shoulders into the hole and looked at the rock blocking the tunnel. Andy reached in and dug at the edges. Dirt came away and dropped to the floor. He scraped away more and soon they could see a definite edge to the rock.

"What have we got to dig with?" he asked.

Trevor turned back to the room and scrounged around until he found an old fork that had been left behind by someone long ago. He handed it to Andy.

Andy began scraping at the junction of the cave wall and the back of the cave. The more he scraped the more excited he got.

"This is definitely not solid rock," he said.

"Can you see the edges?"

"I can on one side," he replied.

Andy dug for several minutes and then backed out and handed the fork to Trevor. "Here, give it a try, my hand is cramping up."

Trevor crawled into the hole and began scraping. After several minutes he backed part way out. "Come in here," he said.

Andy crawled in. There was just enough room for both of them to lie face to face in the tunnel. They shined their headlamps on the edges of the tunnel. "Holy smokes," Andy said, "that's not the end of the tunnel at all. That's a rock that's been put there to block the way."

"But how did they get it in there?" Trevor asked. "It's bigger than the hole. How did they get it through there to block it?"

They laid there looking and thinking. It seemed impossible that someone had maneuvered the rock into the hole and then somehow pulled it up against the hole so tightly.

"Oh my gosh," Trevor gasped. "I know how they got it in there."

"How?" Andy asked.

Trevor turned and looked at his friend bathed in the bright

light of the LED lamp. "They brought it in from the other end. They brought it down the tunnel from the sinkhole at the other end and blocked the hole so no one could get in this tunnel."

Andy's mouth dropped open. "Oh man Trev, you're right. That's the only way. And it fits what we were wondering. Why did this tunnel begin and end at the bottom? The answer is........it doesn't... it begins up on the hill and ends here."

"Do you know what this means," Trevor asked.

"I don't want to think about it, but yeah, I know where you're going. We might, we just might have found the lost tunnel."

"And.....?"

"Don't even say it. You'll jinx us."

Chapter 15

The boys gathered up some of the damp mud on the floor and worked it into the cracks they'd opened in the back of the tunnel.

"I doubt that anyone would be in here looking for a clue like we did, but just in case I think it's a good idea to camouflage the rock as much as we can," Trevor said.

They finished their job and pushed all of the junk back into the hole. Then they walked back out into the sunshine by the front of the cave.

"We're going to have to climb up to the top of the hill and search for the sinkhole," Andy said.

"Yeah, but we can't go climbing around on this hill in shorts and bare feet," Trevor replied.

"We've got to think this out and then come back and do a careful search."

They were full of expectation as they climbed down the front of the hill, walked back to the boat and headed back down the river to the landing.

Trevor was sitting in the front of the boat and kept looking back over his shoulder with a huge grin on his face.

After they loaded the boat they went to Andy's house.

He fired up his computer and began searching US Geological Survey Maps for the right area to look at the hill. It took a lot of scrolling and searching but in a while they'd narrowed the search down to the right place.

"This has to be Bogus Bluff," Trevor said. "This is about where we came out of the west tunnel," he said pointing to a spot on the screen. "And here's the ditch that we came out when we went down the east tunnel."

They zoomed back out a little and began looking at the area

between the two cave entrances. It was a big area with many ditches and ridges. There were several possibilities but none of them were a sure thing.

"We're not going to find it like this," Andy said.

"Well I didn't expect to see an arrow pointing that said "Cave Entrance", Trevor said grinning.

"We know it has to be someplace between the outer two don't we?" Andy asked.

"The other two are pretty straight. I doubt that they'd cross any other cave. The place we're looking for has to be in between the other two entrances. The problem is that we don't know how far up the hill it starts," Trevor said staring at the computer screen.

"I agree," Andy said. "We don't have time to go back today but tomorrow we'll wear long pants and boots and start our search."

They got new batteries for their head lamps and slept at Andy's that night.

The next morning they parked off the road and crossed the fence. They stood there looking up the hill.

"Well how the heck do we get up there?" Andy asked.

Trevor shook his head back and forth. "There's no easy way. Either we have to climb up the front like we have been doing and then try to get up over the top, or we have to go up one side or the other."

"It's not going to be easy any way we do it."

Trevor nodded. "I say let's try the west hillside first. It doesn't look as steep as that east side does. We have to try one or the other."

Andy agreed so they began hiking around the bottom of the hill towards the valley on the west side of the hill. The brush was thick and there were lots of briars and prickly ash. The prickly bushes were one problem but the steepness of the hillside made it even more difficult and they soon had worked up a good sweat. It didn't take long for them to become winded.

73

Andy stopped to wipe sweat from his forehead with his tee shirt tail. "No wonder no one ever found this treasure. I'm beginning to think it might not be worth all the work."

"You'll think different if we find canvass sacks of gold," Trevor said.

"That's a big IF."

Trevor was smaller and probably in better shape than Andy so he took the lead. They were working back into the valley and up the hill at a diagonal. They came to an area that was like a rockslide. There were large flat rocks lying all over the place in a field of gravel and shale. It was tricky walking because the shale was slippery and often went out from under them like an avalanche when they walked across it.

"I wonder if this is the place where that Seifert guy told his relatives to 'look under the big flat rock'?" Trevor said.

"Big flat rock, which one.....there are dozens of them. I think that Indian Burial Cave sounds like a bunch of baloney too. Why in the world would anybody haul their dead chief all the way up here to bury him? They'd have to have a lot more ambition than I have."

Andy was just passing a slab of rock when his feet slipped out from under him and he landed on his belly on the ground. The fall knocked the wind out of him and he lay there kind of stunned. Immediately the sound of a loud buzz started coming from under the flat rock.

"Stay still!" Trevor whispered.

Andy froze. He looked out the corner of his eye and could see back under the rock about a foot. "Oh crap," he whispered.

"Is it?"

"Yes."

"How far back is it?"

Andy turned his head an inch. "It's about a foot under the rock. It's all coiled up. Oh shit, why me?"

"You're a good foot from the hole," Trevor said. "So the snake's almost two feet away."

"Great. How far can they strike?" he whispered.

"Not sure. I've heard about the length of their body. How long does he look?" Trevor whispered.

"Well that doesn't make me feel any better. He looks like he's three feet long at least. It's kind of hard to tell when he's all coiled up like that."

"Well that's not good."

"So tell me you have a plan."

"I'm working on it."

The shale was digging into Andy's belly and legs but he didn't dare try to move to get more comfortable. The snake stopped rattling and just stared at him, its tongue flicking out of its mouth.

"I've got an idea," Trevor said finally.

"How nice, does it have a timeline that gets me out of here sometime before school starts in September?"

"Hey, great ideas take time," Trevor said. "Here's what we'll do. I've got a rock here about the size of a football. I'll get it and sneak up near the hole from the side so he won't see me coming. Then when I count to three I'll drop the rock in front of the hole and you scurry away."

"Scurry?"

"Yeah, scurry."

"That's the best you could come up with?"

"Well, there aren't a lot of options, you have a better idea?"

"No, so I guess I'll scurry."

Trevor snuck to the edge of the flat rock and picked up the stone. When he moved in close the snake became agitated and began to rattle again.

"Don't get too close, he's pissed again," Andy whispered.

"He probably felt my footsteps on the ground. Ok, I can drop it from here. Ok, you get ready and scurry on three."

Trevor counted. "One, Two.."

"Wait wait, go on three or go after three?"

"Go when I say three."

"Ok."

"One, Two, Three!" Trevor dropped the stone at the hole under the rock.

Andy was up on all fours crab walking sideways from the hole as fast as he could go. When he got five feet away he stopped and sat down. His hands were shaking and he was sweating like he'd run a marathon.

Under the slab of rock the snake was rattling up a storm.

"I think he's pretty mad now," Trevor said walking over to Andy.

"Oh that's a real shame. I think I gotta go home and change my boxers."

Trevor began laughing. "Have a little slippage?"

Andy laughed too. "Not really but I wasn't far from it. Jeez, this is turning into a nightmare trying to get up to that dang hill."

"It looks like it flattens out a little up there," Trevor said pointing to an area that looked pretty open of brush. "You go ahead a little way and I'll get a stick and move that rock once you're safe. I don't want to keep that poor snake inside there, he'll starve to death."

"Jeez, you're such a conservationist."

"He didn't hurt us. He probably was lying there napping when your big head dropped down and scared him half to death. There's no reason to kill him."

"Ok, Jack Hannah."

Andy crossed the rockslide area very carefully avoiding any flat rock that had even a hint of an opening under it. Trevor waited until Andy was far away and then pushed the rock away from the flat rock. Then he crossed and caught up with Andy.

"Well onward and upward," he said.

Andy swept his arm forward. "You lead."

Chapter 16

The hill didn't get any easier to climb as they moved on. It was very steep, covered with blown down trees and berry briars and strewn with stones and gravel. The footing was very treacherous. The boys were sweating and panting for breath as they stopped at yet another shale slide.

"Oh great, another snake den," Andy said looking across the slippery looking spot.

"We have to be very furtive," Trevor said. "Let me go first. I'm a little more fleet of foot than you are," Trevor said.

"Furtive... where are you getting these words, like scurry, and furtive?" Andy asked.

Trevor grinned. "I read my friend, and I don't mean fishing magazines."

"Okay, professor, go ahead, be my guest, lead on."

Trevor started working his way across the shale and avoided any flat rocks that looked like they had openings under them. The shale slides gave way under their feet often and they slid or fell to the ground. It was tough going. Trevor's feet went out from under him and he went down hard on a shale slide. He got up and grimaced as he wiped his bloody palm on his pants.

"Fleet of foot..." Andy said grinning, but followed carefully behind. It took a quarter of an hour to get across and then they were nearly at the top of the hill. They worked their way through a patch of briars and finally were standing on fairly level ground near the top of the hill.

"Ok, so we're looking for a low spot that has a hole in it I guess?" Trevor asked.

"I guess so. The other two entrances were in little ditches, so I guess we should look at those too. Want to split up or stay together?"

"We'd cover more ground if we split up," Trevor said. He saw the disappointment in Andy's eyes. "But I think we should stay together. Just in case we encounter another rattlesnake it'd be good to have both of us there."

Andy seemed happy to hear that. "Good idea, you lead."

They worked back toward the ridge at the back of the hill. Andy stayed near the west edge of the hilltop while Trevor looked more near the top. They stayed within sight of each other. Andy spotted a low area that was full of slabs of rock and called Trevor over. They carefully poked around in the swale but it looked pretty solid. They moved on and checked out a ditch that had been cut by rainwater that angled down over the side of the hill.

"Let's look at this pretty careful," Trevor said. "This is a lot like the other two openings."

They scoured both sides of the ditch and found nothing that looked like an opening. Three hours later they'd looked at every possible spot that might hide a cave opening on the west side of the hilltop.

"Nothing," Trevor said. "Either we're wrong about this or the hole is on the other side of the hill on the east."

Andy nodded. His shirt was wet with sweat and he was all scratched up from berry briars and prickly ash. "I'm about done in. Let's head back out to the front of the hill on this side and then get down that way."

Trevor agreed. They split up again and searched the front end of the hill for an opening. They found one suspicious swale but it was as solid as the rest of the hilltop. They finally came out on the end of the hill and sat down to rest.

"This is quite a view," Trevor said looking at the panorama of the river valley spread out below them.

"It kind of makes you feel small."

78

Trevor nodded. "I wonder how many people have sat here and had that same thought?"

"Probably lots," Andy said.

"Do you think we're wasting out time? I mean maybe those stories are just stories. Maybe there is no gold at all."

"I thought that at first," Andy said. "But now that we've found the middle tunnel blocked with a big rock I don't think we're wasting our time. Why would someone go through all the trouble to block that tunnel if there wasn't something in there that they wanted to hide?"

Trevor nodded. "But I keep asking myself, why didn't the Indians or pirates or whoever hid the treasure ever come back and get it?"

"I've wondered about that too," Andy said. "But something could have happened to them that kept them from coming back. We don't know how many Indians supposedly were involved. Maybe years later the ones that hid it were all getting old and it just got forgotten. Maybe they were in another battle later and all got killed. Or the pirates did the same, got killed in another battle or got arrested and sent to prison. It's possible it just was left with the intention of coming back for it and something happened that kept them from doing that. People died pretty young in those days. Life was a lot harder than it is today."

"Or it was never there in the first place," Trevor added.

"Or that too."

"Well, I'm not ready to give up yet. I don't want to tackle the east side right away but in a day or two I think we should come back and look at it," Trevor said.

"I agree. Then if we don't find anything we'll have to decide if maybe we were wrong in the first place. I guess it won't cost us anything to look though."

"We would still have one option though," Trevor said.

"What is that?"

"We could try to dig or blast our way in through the rock that's blocking the tunnel."

"Ouch, that sounds like a lot of work. Let's hope it doesn't come to that."

They got up and worked their way down the front of the hill to the trail and then hiked down to the highway. The trip up and down the front of the hill was getting pretty routine and didn't take them very long anymore.

They drove down the highway a little way and pulled off on the shoulder. "Jeez I think that east side is even steeper than the west side," Trevor said looking up at the hill.

"Wow, that's almost straight up," Andy answered.

They sat there looking for a few minutes. Andy was looking back at Judith's Point hill.

"Hey Trev, look at the other hill there. It's not nearly as steep and if we climbed up on it, we could walk around the ridge and get up to the back end of Bogus Bluff from there. It looks easier than trying to go up the side of this dang mountain."

Trevor nodded. "That's a good idea. It might be a little longer walk but it wouldn't be so steep. Good idea man."

"Stick with me.....I'm full of good ideas."

"I've got a good idea right now......let's go home and get something to eat. I'm about starved to death."

"No kidding, that was a pretty good hike, I think we burned a billion calories each doing that."

Chapter 17

I t was two days later when the boys decided to take a look at the east side of Bogus Bluff. They both had to work the day before and they were both still a little tired out from their last expedition up the hill.

"This looks better," Trevor said as they started up the valley between Bogus Bluff and Judith's Point.

"Yeah, less snakey too," Andy replied.

Trevor took the lead and they followed a deer trail up the middle of the valley. They were at the end of the flat part and started up the hill. The deer trail veered off to the east so the boys struck out to the left so whey could get up on top of Bogus Bluff again, on the east side.

Trevor was setting a pretty good pace and Andy got a little behind. Suddenly he thought that there was movement in the grass. He stopped and looked and definitely saw movement.

"Snake!" he hollered and took off away from the critter.

Trevor came back down a little way and poked around with a stick. A rattling sound came from the grass when he poked into it.

"Another of those dang rattlesnakes," Andy said from a safe distance.

"No, listen to it. That's not the same sound," Trevor said. He moved carefully into the grass and poked with his stick and turned and raised the stick with a large snake dangling from it.

"Are you crazy?" Andy said backing up.

"It's a bull snake," Trevor said. "They twitch their tail in the grass trying to sound dangerous. They're not poisonous."

"How nice to know that Professor. Now put the dang thing

down the hill and let's go."

Trevor tossed the snake a little way down the hill and it moved off through the grass. "If I'd have known I was going treasure hunting with a girl I'd have brought a box of chocolates," he said under his breath.

"Keep it up," Andy said. "It'd be terrible if a big rock happened to fall on your stupid head and crack it open."

Trevor laughed. "You won't get close enough to the rocks to pick one up so I'm pretty safe I think."

They finally got to the top of the hill and spread out to look for an opening. Andy was on top again and found a couple of good looking prospects but neither had any openings in them. He was approaching another when Trevor called up to him.

"Hey I might have something here," he said.

Andy walked closer carefully. "Where are you?"

Trevor's voice came from the middle of a big patch of berry briars. "I'm in here," he said.

"You throw a snake at me and I'm going to shave your eyebrows off while you're sleeping the next time we go camping."

Trevor laughed. "I'm not going to throw a snake. Come down here, this looks good."

Andy cautiously walked closer. The berry briars were really thick and he stopped when he got next to them. "How did you get in there?"

"Go around to the east side. The briars aren't so thick there."

Andy walked to the other side and saw an area where the briars were thinner. He carefully walked into the patch getting grabbed by several of the nasty branches. He was almost in when one particularly big one slapped him across the nose.

"Yeeeeow!" he said.

"Get stuck?" Trevor asked laughing.

"This better be good."

"Hurry up!"

Andy finally could see Trevor standing in the middle of the

briars on a pile of rocks. The ground was pretty open there with just a few briars growing up between the spaces in the rocks.

"Take a look," Trevor said.

Andy looked down where Trevor was pointing. There was a large flat rock lying flat in the bottom of the swale and many other round rocks piled on top of it.

"This isn't a natural pile of rocks," Andy said.

"You're right about that. This is a door and it's been camouflaged by someone with rocks to make it look like it belongs here. The problem is there aren't any other flat rocks within a hundred yards and no other boulders at least that far away. These have been carried here and put here for a purpose."

Andy looked at Trevor and grinned. "To hide something, like a cave entrance?" he asked.

Trevor nodded. "Go to the head of the class."

They began to move some of the rocks and boulders. They cleared out the area over the flat slab of rock. It was about 4 feet on a side and half a foot thick.

"That's got to weigh 5 or 6 hundred pounds," Trevor said.

"At least.....we can't move it without help."

"We don't want to get anyone else up here," Trevor said.

"I didn't mean other people. I mean equipment."

"What's your plan?"

"We've got rental stuff in the store. I'm sure my boss will let me borrow a couple of things. We need a couple of iron bars to pry this up to see if there IS a hole there. And if there is, we need a heavy nylon strap and a come-along to lift it up off the hole."

Trevor grinned. "Good idea. I knew I kept you around for something."

"I know. You need a victim now and then."

"Well you can't beat fun. So what do you think?"

Andy looked down at the slab of stone. "I think someone went through an awful lot of work to get this slab down here and to cover it like this. I think there must be something under it that made it all worthwhile to them."

Trevor nodded. "Let's go. We've got equipment to get."

They worked their way out of the briar patch and Trevor got a good smack on his left ear. Blood was dripping down his neck when they emerged from the briars.

"We need one more piece of equipment," he said.

"And what is that?" Andy asked.

"A pruning shears, to cut a path through those dang briars."

"Good idea," Andy said looking at the blood on Trevor's ear.

Chapter 18

A ndy didn't want to tell his boss that he and Trevor were hunting for treasure so he gave him a story about doing some excavating for a garden spot for his grandpa. His boss was glad to lend him the tools. He hated to lie to the boss but he also felt kind of foolish about telling him they were on a treasure hunt.

The next morning the boys drove out to the hills and parked as usual. They began walking up the valley they'd explored the previous day, carrying the equipment. Andy was carrying the come-along and had a roll of rope slung over his shoulder. Trevor was carrying two iron pry bars, and had the pruning shears in his pocket.

"Jeez, these things weigh a ton," he complained.

"Want to trade? This thing pinches your fingers if you don't carry it just right. I'll switch with you if you want."

"Never mind, I'm good."

They walked slowly up the valley and then up the hillside to the briar patch. Then they carefully made their way into the middle of the briars, snipping off prickly branches that stuck out into the path. They left a few of the higher ones so the path wasn't so noticeable. By bending down a little they had a nice clear path in and out of the briars.

"There," Trevor said, "now we can come and go without getting ripped apart every time."

"Ok," Andy said. "We need a couple of good stable rocks to put our pry bars on to try to lift this big slab. I think once we get it up, one will be able to hold it while the other puts the nylon strap around it."

Trevor agreed and they looked through the rocks and found a couple they thought would work. They placed them about a foot from the edge of the big slab. Andy took the loop of nylon strap from the come-along and spread it out on the side of the slab where they were going to try to lift. Then they each picked up a pry bar and slid them under the slab as far as they could get them. They balanced the pry bars on the rocks they'd placed and they were ready.

"Ok, on the count of three," Trevor said.

"Go on three or one, two, three and then go?"

Trevor laughed. "You just have a problem with that concept don't you? Go on three!"

"Jeez, touchy....I was just asking."

Trevor counted. "One, two, three!"

They both pushed down on their pry bar. The slab of rock moved an inch.

"Push!" Trevor said through gritted teeth.

They each bore down on their pry bar and the stone lifted a couple of inches. Andy leaned across his pry bar with his whole weight and the slab came up another few inches on his side. "Lay on it," he gasped.

Trevor climbed onto his pry bar and the stone lifted a little farther. "No way," he said, "it's too heavy."

They both backed off and let the slab down.

"Whew, that's a heavy stone. I bet it weighs more than we thought."

Andy stood there looking at it. "There's got to be a way."

"How about if we use just one pry bar and both of us on it push on it?" Trevor suggested. "Then we can lay the other here next to the nylon strap and when we get it up a bit we can push the pry bar under, keeping the stone up."

"That might work. What we really need is a fat guy or one more person to push the extra bar under while we pry on it."

Trevor shrugged. "We've got us and that's it. Let's try

anyway." He laid the iron bar next to the slab and they centered one of the lifting stones to the middle of the slab. They put one pry bar under it and started pushing again.

This time the slab rose about three inches. Then Andy put his whole weight on the bar with Trevor pushing and it came up another few inches. "Push the pry bar under!" Andy gasped.

Trevor tried to keep pushing while he moved the bar with his foot. It slid under the slab and they backed off the pry bar. The slab settled on the iron bar and stayed up off the ground about an inch. The iron bar sunk into the ground a few inches on each end but kept the slab from going all the way down flat again.

"Whew," Andy said.

Trevor got down on his belly and crawled to the edge of the slab. He peered under it to the darkness below. He looked into the space and then got up.

He was grinning. "It's there. There's a hole there."

Andy jumped up and down. "Oh man, this might be it."

They both got down on their bellies to take a look. Under the slab there was a hole that had been carved out of the hilltop that was about two feet across. There was dirt around the edges but even from outside the actual hole they could see rock under the dirt.

"It's definitely a cave," Trevor said.

"Pretty small but you're right it's the beginning of a cave, just like the others we found."

They were both shaking with excitement. "Ok we've got to calm down and take this slow and steady," Andy said.

"Right, you're right."

"Ok now what we need to do is find something to anchor this come-along to so we can move this slab of rock."

They stood looking around the briar patch and it didn't look very good.

"There's nothing in here that'd be strong enough," Trevor said.

"You're right. We need a tree or big rock outside of the

briars. There's a pretty long rope with the come-along. I hope it's long enough."

"I'll go out and look," Trevor volunteered.

He moved carefully back through the briars and soon he yelled to Andy. "I found a small oak tree over here."

"Where are you?"

Andy looked and saw a branch waving back and forth on the west edge of the briars. "Perfect," he said. "That's almost exactly in line with the direction we need to move this slab."

"Ok so how do we get the rope through the briars?"

"I was hoping you'd volunteer to crawl through," Andy yelled back.

"Think again, I thought you'd volunteer to crawl through."

"I'm the brains of the operation, you're the brawn."

He could hear Trevor laughing. "I'll meet you half way."

As much as Andy wanted to stay clear of the briars, he agreed. "Ok, see you in the middle."

Andy hooked the nylon strap of the come-along around the slab of rock and then carefully stepped across the pile of rocks to the other edge of the swale. "Where are you?"

"Right here," Trevor responded.

Andy got down on his hands and knees and began crawling through the briars. In just a minute he had a dozen cuts and gashes in his arms and hands, plus one good one across the bridge of his nose. "Are you coming?"

"I'm half way in," Trevor's voice came from a little way away.

Suddenly Andy saw something coming through the briars on the ground. "Holy crap, a damn snake is in here!" he yelled. He began crawling backward with several briars grabbing his clothes and ripping into his skin. A big branch like a small sapling hooked his tee shirt and pulled it up over his head as he crawled backwards.

"No, wait a minute.......look closer," Trevor said laughing.

Andy stopped and looked more carefully and saw the "snake" was just a long stick.

"Tie the rope onto that stick and I'll pull it through," Trevor said.

Andy relaxed a bit. "Jeez why didn't you tell me you were pushing a stick through... I almost pooped my pants."

Trevor was laughing so hard he could hardly answer. "Sorry" he said.

Andy tied the rope to the stick and watched as it disappeared through the briars.

"Got it," Trevor said.

Andy waited.

"Ok, it's long enough, barely. I'll tie it onto the tree and meet you back in the rocks."

Andy began backing out of the briars. Now they were grabbing at his legs and butt cheeks. He was getting shredded.

"Boy," he said to himself, "this better turn out to be worth it, it just better."

Chapter 19

Trevor appeared in the opening and carefully crawled back into the middle of the briar patch. He looked at Andy with alarm and a little snicker.

"Jeez it looks like you got attacked by a herd of cats," he said.

Andy had bleeding cuts all over his arms and a big nasty looking one across his nose and cheek.

"That was a heck of a mess in there," he replied. "Hey wait a minute, why aren't you all cut up too?"

"I used my head for an idea instead of using it like a battering ram like you did," he said. "Did you notice the stick? I only had to get a little way into the briars and then push the stick in to you."

Andy shook his head. "What a pal," he said.

"Well, let's see if this idea is going to work or not," Trevor said.

They stood on either side of the big slab of rock and Andy turned the come-along over so the lever was on top. He took hold of the lever and began working it back and forth tightening the rope that he had tied to the device as he waited for Trevor. After a couple of minutes the rope was taut and the nylon strap began to tighten up. As he worked the lever back and forth the rope tightened more and began to snap and groan.

"It's working," he said.

He kept working the lever and the rock began to scrape as it slid to the side of the hole a tiny bit. Another few cranks on the lever and it wedged against a pile of the smaller rocks and began to rise up.

"The oak tree is just high enough over this ditch that it's going to lift that slab," Andy said smiling as he worked the lever.

"Stay clear," Trevor said. "In case that rope breaks we don't want to have our feet under that slab."

Andy kept working the lever and the slab crept up a little at a time until it was at about a forty five degree angle above the hole.

"Stop there," Trevor said. "Let's get something to prop it up and leave it there for now."

"Why not just tip it all the way over?" Andy asked.

"If we leave it like this, half way open, we can lower it again if we want to. In case we want to hide the hole again."

Andy nodded. "Good idea," he said. "If we drop it over on its back we'd never be able to lift it back up and over the hole again."

They placed two rocks just under the slab where it touched the ground and then placed several more along the first two to make a wall that would hold up the slab. Andy loosed the lever and reversed it and let the slab down carefully on top of the wall of rocks.

Trevor pushed against it to make sure it was stable and the slab didn't move a bit.

"That looks good," he said. "I'd hate to crawl down in that hole and have the slab fall back down. It would not be good."

"No kidding. We'll leave the strap on just in case too. I'd hate to think of being down there and having that thing fall on me."

They knelt down and looked over the edge of the hole. The tunnel dropped down about ten feet and then gradually angled toward the end of the bluff. It was about two feet wide.

"We're going to need a ladder or a rope," Trevor said.

"Yeah, if we crawled down we'd never be able to get back up here. This tunnel is pretty smooth."

"There's another problem. Do you see how narrow it is? How are we going to turn around in it? We might have to go all the way to the end before we can turn around to come back."

"We're going to have to go in head first," Andy said.

"Holy smokes, you're right."

They sat and looked down the dark damp hole. The thought of crawling for hundreds of feet in the dark and finding that they couldn't turn around at the end was pretty terrifying.

"Wow, I didn't expect this," Trevor said.

"Me either," Andy said. "We're going to have to think this over a little bit."

They decided to go home and think about their options and then decide what to do next. They left the cave entrance open thinking that no one would bother it and if they did, they wouldn't go down into that hole without equipment.

That night Andy stayed at Trevor's and they talked long into the night about their dilemma. After several hours of dissecting the problem they decided on a plan.

"I'll go in first," Trevor said. "You stay up on top and lower me down and I'll scout it out. I don't have a problem with that."

"If you're sure," Andy said. "You know... we could just go back and lower the slab and forget about it."

Trevor looked at his friend. "We'd never forget about it Andy. It would haunt us until the day we die. Probably all we'll find is another cave, but if there's even a chance that the treasure is in there, we have to look. Someday when we're old men we'd still wonder if we missed out on the adventure of our lives."

"You're right," Andy replied. "But I'm glad it's you going instead of me."

"Well, you'll be the one all alone in the middle of a rock pile often frequented by snakes."

Andy punched him in the arm.

Chapter 20

They got a roll of rope from Andy's garage. It was a new anchor rope that he'd been trying to get around to putting in the boat, but the cave exploration had kept him from getting to it. They also got their head lamps and put new batteries in them.

When they got back to the hill they climbed up to the briar patch and walked through the entry path.

"That's a lot better now that you trimmed off those grabbing branches," Andy said.

"I kind of hate to make it too open just in case someone stumbles along here and notices the path. They might see our cave and mess this up for us," Trevor said.

"I doubt there are many people just out hiking around here. It's a steep hike up here and there's not much to see once you get here.   There probably won't be any hikers out just meandering around. In any case I'll take the path over being cut to ribbons every time I crawled through there."

Trevor laughed. "We'll heal. If we find a treasure, you can buy lots and lots of healing skin cream."

"Don't say that! You'll jinx us."

Once they were in the middle of the briar patch Andy took the rope and tied it around Trevor's ankles.

"Ok, let me down slow," Trevor said looking over the edge.

"Don't worry, I'll be careful. And even if you got away from me, you'd land on your head and that'd be like landing on a hard rock."

"Funny."

Trevor slid forward and Andy held onto the rope until it tightened.   Then he began to let rope out and he watched Trevor's legs and feet disappear over the edge of the hole. "Keep going," Trevor said from the below.

Andy played out the rope a little at a time and then Trevor

said, "Ok stop, I'm at the bottom."

Andy looked over the hole and watched as Trevor disappeared into the tunnel. He had the rope still tied around his legs. Andy kept letting out rope as Trevor drug it into the hole.

"Are you ok?" he asked.

"Just a second," Trevor replied.

Then the rope moved down the tunnel a quite a bit and Andy watched to see what was happening. "It's getting bigger," Trevor said from inside the tunnel.

Suddenly Andy jumped as Trevor's head appeared in the tunnel opening.

"It goes about ten feet and then it splits... where the two tunnels split off its big enough to turn around. The left tunnel is pretty small, like that one on the east side of the hill but the other one is bigger. We can crawl down that one."

"So you want me to come down?" Andy asked.

"Why don't you find something to tie the rope onto and then climb down and join me? You'll have to back in but it's not far. I'll wait for you where the tunnels split and we can explore them one at a time."

"Ok, be right back," Andy said.

He made sure there was plenty of rope down the hole and then took the rest back through the opening in the briars and tied it to a maple that was a short way away. He made sure the knot was good and tight and then he made his way back into the briars. He looked down into the hole and took a deep breath.

"Well, here goes," he said.

He slipped over the edge and hung onto the rope and let himself down to the bottom.

"I can see your feet," Trevor said. "Just get down and back in."

Andy stuck his feet into the tunnel and backed up until he felt Trevor's hands on his shoes.

"Ok, just another couple feet and then you can sit up."

Andy moved back in and sat down on the damp floor.

Trevor's head lamp was shining in his eyes. He put his hand up to shield his face.

"Oops sorry," Trevor said turning his head.

"Take a look."

Andy turned on his head lamp and looked where Trevor was pointing. The tunnels did indeed split just ahead of them. The left one was twenty inches to two feet wide and headed back a long way. The right one was maybe three feet across and it too went as far as their lights would shine.

"What do you think?" Andy asked.

"I think we need to check both of them out. The only thing with this left one is if we get in there and don't find an exit, we'll have to back all the way out."

"Eww, that would be a bummer," Andy said.

"I think only one of us should go," Trevor said. "It'd be a lot easier for one to do it and then back out. If we find something we both can go back in."

"Sounds like a good plan to me."

"So you or me?"

"How about rock, paper, scissors?"

"Ok, on three."

"Show on three or three and then show?"

"Jeez you really have a problem with go-on-three don't you?" Trevor laughed. "Three and show."

"Ok just checking."

They each made a fist and Trevor counted, "One, Two, Three!"

Trevor laid out a flat palm and Andy made a fist.

"Paper covers rock, you go."

"Two out of three?"

"Go you weenie," Trevor laughed.

Andy took a deep breath. "Ok if I start yelling, you come and get me."

"I promise," Trevor answered.

Chapter 21

Andy started down the tunnel on his belly. He had to scoot forward on his elbows and push with his toes as they had done in the east tunnel. The floor was damp and muddy. He kept his light shining ahead making sure he was ready for anything that might be down there.

The tunnel seemed to be going downhill. It was hard to tell but he felt his head was lower than his feet most of the time. After what seemed like a quarter an hour he stopped for a breather. He looked up at the rock roof of the tunnel.

"Holy smokes... just think of all the rock and dirt that's up there on top of me," he thought to himself. "What the heck am I doing? It didn't seem so spooky when Trevor was with me."

He started out again and now he was sure he was going downhill. The angle was definitely getting steeper. '

"How's it going?" Trevor's voice echoed down the tunnel.

Andy jumped and cracked his head on the roof.

"Ow, jeez... You scared me half to death!" he yelled back to Trevor.

"Sorry, find anything yet?"

"It's pretty much like the east tunnel except I think I'm going downhill."

"That makes sense... the other tunnels went uphill from the front."

Andy moved on and soon he saw a void in the floor of the tunnel."

"Hold it... I might have something here," he shouted.

He moved forward a few feet and found himself at the edge of a drop that went straight down into the earth. The tunnel took a right angle drop to the bottom of the hill apparently.

"There's a big hole here. The tunnel goes on but it goes straight down. We aren't going any farther here," he shouted.

"Can you see the bottom?"

Andy scooted forward and leaned over the chasm. His light shined down many feet but he couldn't see the bottom of the tunnel. He looked around and found a pebble and dropped it. He waited for about three seconds and then heard it hit.

"It's deep, way way deep."

"Come on back," Trevor yelled.

"You don't have to tell me twice," Andy yelled back.

He began scooting backward and it was much more difficult than going forward. His shirt rolled up under him and soon he was mud from the top of his jeans to his chin. His elbows were getting sore and his toes began cramping up.

He kept working backward and suddenly he heard Trevor's voice.

"I can see your light. You've got about twenty yards or less."

"Oh yippie," Andy said.

Finally he felt Trevor's hands grab his ankles and pull him back into the main tunnel. He sat up and turned back to Trevor.

"Holy cow, you look like a mud pie," Trevor said laughing.

"I feel like I've been shot at and missed and shit at and hit," Andy said. He grinned and his teeth shone white as snow against his mud covered face.

"You definitely need a little rinse," Trevor said.

"I think I've had about enough of dark damp places for one day," Andy said to his buddy.

"I agree, we'll come back tomorrow and look at the other tunnel. I think that one is a much better chance of being the place we're looking for anyway."

"What? Why did we look at this one then?"

"We want to be thorough, don't we?"

"Yeah, I guess. Tomorrow, you're going in then. No more rock, paper, scissors."

Trevor grinned. "No problem."

They crawled to the end of the tunnel and Trevor slipped out into the hole and pulled himself up the rope. Andy followed and got to the top right after Trevor.

"We might as well leave it as is," Trevor suggested.

"I doubt anybody will be up here snooping around."

They hiked down the hill to the jeep. When they got there Trevor looked at Andy.

"Um, I hate to say this but you're covered with mud. How about jumping in the river and cleaning yourself off before you get in my jeep? You can clean your clothes off and then we'll throw them in the back where they won't destroy my seats."

Andy looked at him. "And then what... ride home naked?"

Trevor shook his head. "As much as I'd enjoy that, I have some clothes in the back from the other day when we went swimming. My swimming suit is there. You can put that on."

Andy grinned. He walked down over the riverbank and took off his shoes. Then he removed his head lamp and took a mighty leap and jumped into the river. He surfaced and took off his clothes and tossed them up on the shore. Then he rubbed himself down washing the mud off.

Trevor retrieved his clothes, rinsed them off in the water and tossed them in the back of the jeep. He came back with his swimming shorts. Andy waded out and wiped himself off as best he could with his hands and put on the swimming shorts.

"There, satisfied?" he asked.

"You're a prince among men," Trevor replied.

Chapter 22

A ndy was pretty sore from his trip down the skinny tunnel so they took a day off from cave exploring. They both had to work the afternoon shift anyway, so the following day they headed back up to the cave.

They had a pretty good path up the valley and then up the hillside so it took less time every day they went back up the hill. They arrived at the briar patch and waded through. Andy climbed down first and then Trevor followed him, backing into the hole until they could sit up in the larger space.

Andy was looking around when Trevor backed in.

"Hey, this looks like someone chipped it out and made it bigger," he said pointing to the walls and ceiling. It's like the room at the other end."

Trevor looked and nodded. "You're right. Somebody made this so they could get in and out easier. Good call."

"Well," Trevor said. "I guess it's up to me to go down this one."

Andy shrugged. "If you insist... as much as I'd like to do it, I did promise you the other day that this one was yours."

Trevor started crawling down the tunnel. It was large enough that he could crawl along pretty easily. The tunnel went straight for a long way and then seemed to veer to the left a tiny bit. 'It looks like it's going for the middle of the hill, which is where it might meet the big room," he thought to himself.

After crawling for a long way he noticed chips of rock lying in the mud. Some of them were buried and some just sticking out of the mud. "Looks like somebody chipped some stuff away," he thought. "This mud must come down here when it rains hard. This stuff was chipped a long time ago and that's why it's buried."

"Find anything?"

Andy's voice came echoing down the tunnel.

"Nothing yet... I must be getting close to the other end though."

Trevor went another several yards and then stopped in his tracks. In front of him was a pile of rocks the size of basketballs. They were piled up and blocked the tunnel completely. The tunnel had been widened out so a slab of rock could be placed up against the smaller end of the tunnel. This was the other side of the rock at the back of the big room on the front of the hill.

"Andy, I found the end. It's blocked with rocks."

"See any treasure?"

"Nope."

There was a long pause. "You want me to come and look too?"

"I think we need to pull some of these rocks away to see what's under them. Yeah, why don't you come down too?"

"Ok, I'm on my way."

Trevor sat down and looked around him. The rocks had been carefully placed and were definitely carried there. He began to move a few to the side as he waited.

Several minutes later he heard Andy coming down the tunnel. He saw his light coming and soon Andy was sitting beside him looking at the rock pile.

"It's just like we thought. I bet if we pull enough of those rocks away we could drop that slab of rock and go out into the front room of the cave," he said.

Trevor nodded. "I was thinking the same thing."

They started pulling rocks from the big pile and began placing them along the side of the tunnel. It didn't take long and they saw exactly what they were expecting. There was a flat slab of stone up against the tunnel held in place by the rocks. The slab was just slightly smaller than the diameter of the tunnel they'd just crawled down.

They sat down and rested. Andy checked the edges of the slab and nodded.

"It's been chipped away so it would fit down the hole and down this tunnel. So now we know that someone blocked this tunnel to hide something," Andy said.

"We're hoping they blocked it to hide the gold."

"Ok, so where is it then?"

Andy shook his head. "Did you see anything on the way in that looked like a place to hide it?"

"No, but I wasn't really looking either," Trevor said.

"What do you suppose we're looking for? I mean, I wonder how much gold it would be? The story is that it was gold coins so how many would there be?" Andy asked.

"It depends on if the Astor gold is here, or the Spanish gold or the US gold, or all of them. It doesn't take much room to hide a lot of dollars worth of gold. Even in those days a small sack would hold a fortune."

"So it probably wasn't in a treasure chest," Andy said.

"It might have been on the boat, but I'm sure it was probably in bags and the Indians or pirates took it out of the chest and carried it up here a bag at a time. A bag of gold coins would weigh several pounds I guess. They wouldn't try to carry it all up here in one big box. That would be too hard."

Andy nodded. "Ok, so we're looking for cloth bags, or probably canvas bags."

"Maybe it's in the original bags or maybe they dumped it out someplace and buried it in jars or pottery, or who the heck knows."

"Well you're a real wet blanket," Andy said.

Trevor laughed. "I just meant we have to keep our minds open. We can't go looking for canvas bags or a wooden box and overlook something else."

Andy looked at the pile of rocks. "You don't suppose it's under all of those rocks at the door do you?"

"If you went through all the trouble to block the end of the tunnel, and the work of carrying all of those rocks way down here would you hide your gold right there?"

Andy shook his head, "You're right. It would be too obvious. I'd hide it back here farther. Or, maybe in the other tunnel or... oh I hate to say this... maybe they dropped it down that hole."

"They didn't steal it so they could just drop it down a hole. They planned on spending it don't you think?"

"Maybe they know where that hole comes out at the bottom of the hill."

Trevor looked at his pal. "If they had a hole at the bottom of the hill that they could get into to retrieve the gold, why would they climb all the way up here, block this tunnel off, and then drop the gold back down to the bottom?"

"Good point."

"Well, let's work our way back out and look along the way for clues," Andy said.

Trevor nodded. "We might have crawled right past it."

Chapter 24

Andy was in front and Trevor brought up the rear as they worked slowly back down the tunnel. They looked up at the ceiling and the walls and looked carefully at the mud on the bottom of the tunnel.

They'd gone about half way when Andy dug something out of the mud. He wiped it off and turned to Trevor and showed him what he'd found.

"Look at this," he said.

Trevor took a piece of shell with a hole drilled through it from his hand. "It looks like some kind of decoration an Indian might have worn. Maybe it was from a necklace that broke while they were in here."

Andy nodded. "At least it makes me think Indians were here once."

They kept crawling and soon were noticing chips of rock in the mud. "I saw this on the way in," Trevor commented. "I thought they might have made some excavations but I didn't see anything."

Andy looked carefully at the rock chips. "They definitely look like they've been chipped from the walls... but why?"

They moved on a bit and Andy stopped and picked up something from the floor. It was material of some kind.

"Hey look at this," he said.

Trevor took the small piece of cloth from him. It was heavy and very rotten. It almost fell apart in his hands.

"This is old canvas," he said. "I bet it's from one of the bags that the gold was in. It probably rotted away in this damp air. I bet it was white once, but now it's almost black with mold."

"Here's another piece," Andy said picking up another scrap of the canvas.

They carefully looked at the floor and soon found several more small pieces of the cloth. Some were buried in the mud and just barely showing.

"This is important," Trevor said looking around. "There's a reason this is here, we just have to figure it out."

Andy reached in his pocket and took out his jackknife. He began scraping the mud away from the floor. In places the mud was a couple inches deep and in others it was nearly clear of mud. The two of them began sorting through the mud, checking it out for any other clues.

Suddenly Trevor gasped. Andy looked at him and he had a small object in his fingers. He began wiping the mud from it. Then he rubbed it on his shirt and they both inhaled.

"It's a coin!" Trevor said.

"It's a gold coin!"

Trevor cleaned the small coin off. He turned it over in his fingers.

"Oh my gosh Andy," he said. "It says, *Napoleon Empereur.*"

"Napoleon Bonaparte was the emperor of France.....holy cow it's one of the French coins."

Trevor turned the coin over. "On the back is says 20 Francs and the date is 1812."

His hand was shaking as he handed the nickel sized coin to Andy. "The story IS true."

Andy looked at the coin. On the back it said *Empier Francais,* the Empire of France. There was a laurel wreath on it like they used to put on the winners in the Olympics and on the front there was a man with the wreath on his head. "You suppose that's Napoleon?" he asked.

"I have no idea, but I know one thing. We've done something that people have been trying to do for nearly 200 years. We found the gold."

"We found one coin," Andy said. "I hate to be a spoil sport but that's not a treasure."

"But it's a start buddy," Trevor said grinning.

"You got that right."

"Let's scratch this mud up and see if we can find any more."

Andy began scratching the mud and Trevor came behind him sorting through it. "I'm going to look here where we found that canvass. I'm thinking one of the bags leaked or broke open and they lost a few coins. The rest are here someplace."

Five minutes later Trevor found a second coin and then Andy dug one up with his knife. They searched every square inch of the floor in the area but there were no more coins.

"Hmm, only three of them," Andy said. "There's got to be more."

"I agree, but right now I'm stumped as to where they might be."

"Me too," Andy said.

"Let's take these and look them up online. Then we've got to put on our thinking caps and figure out where the rest of them are," Trevor said.

"You're right about that."

They crawled along the floor the rest of the way out with a lot more energy than they'd had going in. When they got to the entrance they climbed up the rope and then took a look at the coins in good light. '

"Wow, they're just like brand new," Andy said examining the shining coins.

"They probably were minted and then lost. They most likely were never in circulation. I wonder if they're worth something more than the value of the gold as rare coins that a collector would want?"

"I bet they are, but even if they're not, the gold in them is worth a lot. It's over a thousand dollars an ounce I think."

Andy tossed one of the coins in his hand. "I have no idea how heavy that is. It's heavier than a nickel, that's for sure."

Trevor put his arm around his buddy's shoulder. "Let's go and find out, I can tell you one thing, we're richer than we were a little while ago."

The two friends nearly ran down the hill back to the jeep.

Chapter 25

The boys were in Andy's bedroom at the computer. Andy typed in the words, French Coin Napoleon, into Google and a list of websites came up.

"Look at that one," Trevor said pointing to one of them.

Andy clicked on the site and there was a coin that looked exactly like the ones they had found. Andy began reading, "Minted from 1804 to 1814. Fineness: .900, with a weight of .1867 troy ounces."

"What's a troy ounce?" Trevor asked.

Andy typed it in the search engine.

"It says it's an ounce. Well that's helpful. Why not just say ounce?" Then he read farther. "It says something about some other kind of measurement but in the end it means an ounce is an ounce."

Trevor laughed.

"Ok, so one coin is about 1/5 ounce… look up what gold is worth."

Andy typed it in and said, "Wow, $1,575.40 per ounce right now."

Trevor was staring off into space and then he turned and said, "That means there's over $300 worth of gold in one of these coins."

"Holy smokes, nearly a thousand dollars for the three of them?" Andy exclaimed.

"Plus I bet the fact that they're like brand new and 200 years old makes them even more valuable," Trevor added.

They sat there stunned. Three little pieces of metal were worth hundreds of hours of them working at the hardware store or grocery store. They'd have to work nearly all summer to make that much money.

"Let's look for a place to take them to see for sure," Trevor suggested.

Andy typed in Coin Dealer into the search engine and there were thousands of them. "Try Wisconsin dealers," Trevor said.

Andy modified the search and there were still several hundred listed. They looked through them and saw a couple in Madison.

Trevor pointed to one of them. "I know about where that is," he said. "It's near the basketball stadium."

"What do you think? Should we make a trip to Madison and see what they'll give us for them?"

Trevor grinned. "Why not? We can't spend them like they are."

The next day they headed to Madison and soon were driving down the street where the Coin Shop was suppose to be. Trevor suddenly pointed to the right and there it was, Capital City Coin and Gold.

They parked and went into the store. There was no one behind the counter so they stood there waiting.

"Kinda junky," Trevor said under his breath. The place was cluttered with all kinds of what looked mostly like junk. There were a lot of musical instruments, used computers, bikes, and a glass case full of coins and jewelry.

Andy nodded. "A lot junky, maybe this place isn't where we should try."

Just then an old man came out from the back room. He was heavy-set, and nearly bald with thick glasses and about a three day growth of beard. He was wearing what once was a white shirt but now was a shade of gray, suspenders and baggy dress pants. He had a stained tie hanging loose around his neck.

"Hello there gentlemen," he said. "How may I help you today?"

"Hello, we were wondering if you might be able to give us an idea of what these are worth?" Trevor said laying the coins on the counter.

The man looked down and his eyes got big. He scooped up

the coins and took a little magnifying glass from the counter and looked at them through it. He examined each coin very carefully.

"Where did you boys get these?" he asked.

"Why" Andy asked.

"Oh, I'm just curious. These are very rare coins. They're 200 years old and look like they've never been in circulation. There are no scratches or wear on them. You don't find something like this every day you know."

"We found them," Andy said.

"Found them did you?"

Andy nodded. "So can you tell us what they're worth?"

The man reached under the counter and pushed a button and a man appeared from the back room. The boys looked at him and nearly ran from the store. He was very tall, well over six feet, his head was shaved and his face very thin and bony. His skin was nearly white as chalk and he was dressed all in black.

"Voldemort." Trevor whispered.

Andy snorted and began to giggle.

"My associate, Mr. Gardens," the shop owner said. He passed the coins to the black man who looked at them as the shop owner had. He took a little magnifying glass out and checked them very carefully. Then he took a little cloth and polished each coin before looking at them again under magnification. He looked at the boys and said, "Lovely, are there more?"

The man's eyes were as black as his clothes. His voice was very deep and he had a strange accent.

"This is all we found," Trevor said avoiding looking at the man.

"You didn't tell me where you found them," the first man said.

"We helped tear down an old shed and they were under the floor," Andy lied.

"I see, well I'd look around very carefully for more," he said, "You see, these sell for....oh in the neighborhood of $300 each," the shop owner said.

"Three hundred each?"

"Yes, the market varies with the price of gold. But of course coins as fine as these would never be melted down for the gold content. I could give you $250 each for them."

The boys looked at each other. "Let us have a minute," Andy said.

They walked out onto the street and Trevor said. "If he wants them for $250 they're probably worth $350."

"Yeah, I thought of that too. But what will we do with them if we don't sell them to him?"

"E-bay?"

"We can do that?"

"I don't know but they sell everything on there, why can't we? Or we can take them to another coin dealer. This guy looks pretty shady to me."

"Ok, let's get the coins and leave."

They walked back into the store.

"We decided we're going to just keep them," Trevor said.

"Really? I could up the offer to $275 each."

"No I think we'll take them home," Andy said.

"You have to understand," Voldemort said, "we have to make a profit on things so we can't give you the full amount they're worth."

"Yeah, we understand," Andy said.

The man held the coins in his hands as if he had no intention of giving them back.

"I'll give you $900 cash... $100 bills."

Trevor looked at Andy. Andy nodded.

"Ok, you've got a deal."

The man nodded to Voldemort and he went to the back room and came out with 9 one hundred dollar bills and counted them out on the counter.

The store owner took out a form and began filling it in. "I need your names and addresses for the transaction."

"Why do you need our names?" Andy asked.

"It's just a common practice, just in case the coins are stolen or fake," the man said.

"Do you have to have both our names? Trevor asked.

"No, just the owner of the coins," the man replied.

"Ok, well my name is Augerhandle, Harry Augerhandle," Trevor said.

The man looked at him.

"Augerhandle is it?"

"Yes," Trevor said, "It's un-hyphenated. A lot of people hyphenate it but it's just straight Augerhandle."

Andy snorted.

"Ok Mr. Augerhandle, where do you live?"

"Steuben, route QQ rural Steuben," Trevor said. Andy turned away trying to keep from bursting out laughing.

"We're pretty rural out in the Steuben area but if you mention the Augerhandle name around there, everybody knows me," Trevor said smiling brightly.

The man wrote the information down and smiled.

"Ok boys, it's been wonderful doing business with you. If you find any more coins like that please bring them here. I'll be happy to buy them from you."

They picked up their money and turned to go.

"Will do," Andy said.

They were getting in the jeep when Trevor noticed Voldemort standing on the sidewalk with a note pad in his hand. He was writing something on the pad.

"What do you think that creepy guy is doing?" he asked Andy.

"Suppose he's taking down our license plate?"

"I hope not."

"Well Harry, let's stop someplace and have lunch, I'll let you buy since you're so rich now."

Trevor laughed. "Harry Augerhandle... do you think he bought it?"

"Not for a minute."

Chapter 26

"**D**id you get it?"

Voldemort nodded.

"We need to figure out where those kids got those coins. They've never been in circulation. Where is this Steuben place?"

"It's west of here, on the Kickapoo river I think. It's in Crawford County."

"On the Kickapoo river... we need to do some research."

"I'll call my friend at the DMV and get the plate information. I know that name was fake and I'd bet they don't live in Steuben either. We'll find them though."

Andy spread out the 9 one hundred dollar bills like a hand of playing cards and fanned himself with them.

"Holy smokes, can you believe this? We got nine hundred dollars for three of those coins?"

Trevor grinned. "That's amazing. I had no idea they'd be worth so much."

"We have to get back up there and figure out if they're the only ones," Andy said.

Trevor nodded. "You got that right."

"What did you think of that guy at the coin store?"

"He gave me the creeps," Trevor said. "When he came out and looked at us, I felt my back pocket to see if my wallet was still there."

"And that black guy... Mr. Gardens. Yikes, he's a scary dude," Andy said.

"You mean Voldemort?"

Andy laughed. "I almost crapped when you whispered that to me."

"I wonder what they're up to?" Trevor said. "I mean they

needed all of our information and then He-Who-Shall-Not-Be-Named took down our license number."

"They're up to no good... that's for sure."

They stopped at a McDonalds and splurged on double quarter-pounders since they were so suddenly rich. Then they headed home.

They were both thinking about the cave and trying to figure out the secret to finding the rest of the gold... if it existed.

"Maybe we should get some of those garden trowels, and go up there and scrape up all that mud and take it out and sift through it," Trevor suggested.

Andy nodded. "Good idea. We found three coins in a little area with a jackknife, maybe the floor is covered with them under the mud. At $300 a coin, I'm willing to do some work to find them."

"How many do you think there might be?" Trevor asked.

Andy shook his head. "I've been wondering about that too. The story goes that they had enough gold to buy furs for a whole year. It had to be a lot of money. How many furs would one of those coins buy?"

"I checked the other day and the internet says that gold was less than $50 an ounce in the early 1800's... so one of those coins would be maybe $10 or so. How much was a beaver worth then?"

"I don't know... a dollar or two?"

"That's what I thought. So some trapper would bring in a few hundred beaver, some mink, some otter, some fox and who knows what else... he might take home quite a few of those coins."

"So there must have been hundreds of them," Trevor said.

"I have no idea, but there had to be a lot of coins to last that long. They were buying furs that trappers all over the area caught so there could have been thousands of them. I don't think anyone else has been in there to find them. If they're not there anymore, the Indians came back and got them long ago. If the Indians didn't come back and get them, we're going to find them."

They both had big grins on their faces as they pulled into Muscoda. They drove up to the hardware store where Andy worked and went right to the garden section, to buy some tools.

"I searched French Napoleons," Gardens said to his boss. "I found something very interesting."

"Oh?... Tell me."

"First the kid's name isn't Augerhandle but Ingalls and he lives in Muscoda. I got his name and address from my friend at the DMV. Muscoda is on the Wisconsin River so I searched French Bonaparts and Wisconsin River and found something that looks good.

Gardens brought up the article on the computer. He moved aside so his boss could see the screen. "It's from an old newspaper story in the Milwaukee Journal from 1922. It tells of a place called Bogus Bluff which is one of a series of high bluffs overlooking the Wisconsin River near Muscoda where there is supposedly a treasure of gold hidden. There are actually several stories, one of American gold coins that were on their way to Fort Crawford to pay the soldiers, one of Spanish Doubloons on their way to New Orleans and this one caught my eye... French Bonaparts being shipped down the river by the American Fur Company to buy a year's worth of furs at Prairie du Chien. John Astor had a fur trading post in Prairie back then. The people delivering the gold were attacked by Indians and the treasure stolen and hidden in the caves at this Bogus Bluff."

"Very interesting... French Napoleons... does it say when this all happened?"

Gardens smiled, "Early 1800's," he said.

"And these coins are 1812," his boss said. "They were probably just minted and this was the first time they'd been used. That would account for them being in such pristine condition."

"Do you suppose those kids found the treasure?"

"Those coins have never been in use. They're as fine as any I've ever seen. So they've been somewhere for the last 200 years where no one has touched them. Where would coins keep better than hidden in a cave?"

Gardens nodded. "So what do we do?"

"I think you need to take a little trip to this Muscoda place and see what you can find out."

"How far should I go to... locate the coins?"

"If there is a year's worth of gold coins there would have to be hundreds of them... maybe thousands. At over $300 each, there could be millions of dollars worth. I think to the right dealers they might be worth $350 to $400 each so we might be talking several million dollars."

Gardens raised his eyebrows. "So whatever it takes?"

The boss nodded.

Chapter 27

"We need a couple of trowels, maybe a little garden claw-thing, to scratch up the mud... what else?" Andy asked.

"We can get some buckets at home. What about a strainer of some kind... maybe it would work to take the buckets down to the river and wash the mud through a colander."

"Good idea, we've got those in the kitchen section."

Soon they had the tools they thought they'd need and they paid for them with some of the change from McDonalds. They drove to Andy's house and went to his room.

"Ok we need to hide the rest of this money," he said.

"Yeah, I feel unsafe walking around with all of that, where can we put it?"

Andy grinned and picked up a trophy that he'd gotten in grade school. He began turning the top of the thing and soon it popped off revealing a hollow base. He took the 8 hundred dollar bills, rolled them up, put a rubber band around them and stuffed them into the trophy, screwed the top back on and set it back on his dresser.

"No one would look at that thing," he said.

"For sure... and nobody would steal it that's for sure."

"Hey, I worked hard perfecting my middle school high

jumping skills to win that trophy."

"Sorry, I thought it was one of those trophies they give to everyone for...you know... participation. I didn't know it was so precious to you."

"I don't like your attitude towards my athletic skills," Andy said trying to look hurt.

"I'm very impressed. Are you happy now? Ok, so tomorrow first thing, let's go up and take a couple of buckets and fill them," Trevor suggested.

That night Trevor stayed over and they talked long into the night about the coins and what their chances were of finding them. The next morning they were up bright and early hiking up the hill with their tools.

They got to the entrance hole and dropped the buckets and tools down and then Trevor climbed down, backed into the tunnel and dragged one bucket with some of the tools inside with him. Andy followed and brought the second bucket along.

They crawled down the tunnel to the end where it was blocked.

"Ok, I'll scratch the mud up with this claw thing, and you scoop it into a bucket. When one is full we'll switch jobs," Trevor said.

Andy was fine with that so Trevor scratched up a patch of mud and then moved aside so Andy could get on the other side of the mud and begin to scoop it into the bucket. Trevor moved backwards down the tunnel towards the end they'd come in from and kept scratching the mud while Andy gathered it up. When one bucket was full, they switched buckets and jobs. The mud was thin in some places but pretty thick in others so it didn't take long to fill both of the buckets. They left the tools where they'd stopped and crawled out of the tunnel each carrying a bucket.

Andy went up the rope first and Trevor tied first one and then the other bucket to the rope while Andy pulled them up. Then Trevor climbed up and they each picked up a bucket and started down the hill.

"I'm nervous as heck," Trevor said.

"Yeah, me too, I'm almost scared to see if we found anything."

Suddenly Andy stopped dead still.

"What?" Trevor asked quietly.

"Something slithered," Andy said.

"Slithered away or toward you?"

Andy turned and grinned, "Away I guess, but you can never be too careful."

Trevor took the lead and they made it down the hill without any further slithering.

They stopped and picked up the colander and climbed down over the river bank. They took off their shoes and waded into the shallow water. Andy held the colander and Trevor shoveled scoops of mud into it. Then Andy lowered it into the river and sloshed it around washing off the mud.

When the first few trowels full were washed they had nothing but a few pebbles left in the colander. They washed the whole first bucket with nothing to show for it.

"Dang, that's not good," Trevor said rinsing out the bucket.

"Not what I hoped for," Andy replied.

They started on the second bucket. The first couple of trowels of mud yielded several rock chips and a few scraps of the black rotten cloth. Andy dumped them and they shoveled more mud into the colander. Andy lowered it into the river, sloshed it around and when he raised it up they both gasped.

"Holy smokes," Andy said picking three more coins from the colander.

"Another $900," Trevor said.

They grinned like mad as they washed off the coins. Andy put them into his pocket and they shoveled more mud into the colander. This time they got more chips, more cloth and two more coins. They ended up with 11 coins when they'd emptied the bucket.

They waded to the bank and sat with their feet in the water

admiring the coins. Each was identical to the others. They were all exactly the same thing as they'd found the first day.

"Ok we figured out something here I think," Andy said.

"The coins are in the mud."

"Nope, the mud near the blocked end was without coins. The mud where we found rock chips and rotten cloth contained the coins. That's the same area where we found the first coins."

Trevor nodded. "You're right, the rock chips and rotten cloth are the keys."

Andy smiled. "And I think I know how it fits together."

"Are you going to let me in on the secret?" Trevor asked.

"Tomorrow, we'll go back up there and I think I can show you where the main treasure is."

"Tomorrow… bull crap… tell me now."

"Be patient Grasshopper."

Chapter 28

That night they stashed the coins with their $100 dollar bills. It was very exciting to see them spread out on the bed next to the pile of cash.

"We've got over $4,000 here," Andy said shaking his head.

"Who'd ever think that something so small is worth so much?" Trevor said picking up one of the coins and turning it in his fingers. "Just think the last person who touched this has probably been dead for nearly 200 years."

"You've got to tell me what your secret is," Trevor said. "I'll never be able to sleep if you don't."

Andy grinned. "The rotten cloth obviously comes from the canvass bags the coins were in when they were stolen by the Indians. Like I said before, they didn't try to carry a big heavy box up the hill with all the gold inside it, but rather they unloaded it and each one carried up a sack or two. I have no idea how big the sacks were but if each coin weighs about 1/5 ounce, there would be 5 coins per ounce. Take that times 16 and there are 90 coins in a pound."

"A roll of quarters is 40 coins, so it'd be like two rolls of quarters," Trevor said.

"Right... and a good sized bag could probably hold say... ten pounds of gold, or 900 coins."

"Holy smokes, you think there are that many up there?"

"I think there are many sacks with 900 or maybe 1,000 coins in each sack. Remember this was the money for a whole year buying furs. There could be lots of sacks. We won't know until we search for them."

Trevor just sat there. "So for all we know there could be 10,000 coins or more. That'd be... $350,000!"

"Multiply that again. I think you missed a zero."

Trevor grabbed the calculator and punched in the numbers.

DAN BOMKAMP

"Oh my sweet baby Jesus, that's $3,500,000... three and a half million dollars!"

Andy nodded. "If there are as many coins as I think there are we're going to be very rich my friend."

Trevor was flabbergasted. "But what if... who's money is it? What happens if somebody comes along and says it belongs to them?"

"Who's going to claim it? The American Fur Company has been gone for 180 years. Astor died a short time after this happened. His heirs may be around but I'm not sure. Even if they are still alive they're billionaires and a few million wouldn't be worth the effort. The Indians couldn't claim it because they stole it in the first place. If they were going to go retrieve it they'd have done so long ago. Most likely the ones who stole it were killed or died afterward in other battles and their secret died with them."

"What about the guy who owns the land?" Trevor asked.

"Well, if we find the treasure, I think we should share with him."

Trevor nodded. "I agree. So how do you know where it is?"

Andy grinned.

"Either you're going to tell me or I'm going to put you in a Full Nelson and squeeze until you do," Trevor said.

"Ok, physical force is not required," Andy said grinning. "In addition to the cloth there are the rock chips. They're not stones that are there naturally. They're sharp and look like they've been chipped from the cave floor or walls. I think the Indians chipped out little niches for each bag or each couple of bags and stashed the bags in them. Remember in the cave room where we first went? They carved little niches into the rock to store things. I think this is what they did here too, to hide the gold. Then they probably smeared some mud over them and they were hidden. Anyone going into the cave would be watching the floor so they didn't step on something or drop into a hole. Few people would look up and if they did, they probably wouldn't

120

have seen the hidden bags."

"Ok, I can believe that but what about the coins in the mud?"

"The coins in the mud came from one of the bags or maybe a couple of them. The cloth rotted and one of the bags was partly exposed by the mud falling off. Maybe it wasn't completely covered in the first place. Someone didn't do a good job of camouflaging the hiding place. If the hole wasn't sealed completely the cloth probably rotted over the years. A bit of the cloth fell away and a few coins dropped to the floor of the cave. A big rain came along and a rush of water ran down the tunnel and the coins were spread around and covered with mud from the rain running down the briar hole and into the top of the tunnel."

Trevor nodded in agreement. "You're a genius. That's got to be what happened!"

"I know I'm a genius, and thanks for acknowledging that. I'm dang good looking too."

"Don't pat your self on the back too hard," Trevor said laughing. "So what's the plan tomorrow?"

"I think we should go in and check the roof and sides of the tunnel. If we find evidence of the rock being messed with, we hammer at it until we find the hidden little nook. Once we find the bulk of the coins, we can still clean all of the mud off the floor to get any coins that may have dropped over the years."

"You think the little niches are at the top?"

Andy nodded. "I think they made their hiding places along the top of the side wall or in the roof. They probably enlarged existing little depressions that were there naturally. If they made them in the floor the next rain would have exposed the sacks of coins."

"That makes sense," Trevor said. "There are many bumps and depressions in the wall that were formed naturally when the cave was formed. They probably used them when they could. We'll see if we can find the hidden ones and then afterward we can sift through the mud on the floor for any that dropped down over the years. At $300 each I'll scoop mud all day long. Wow, now I'm really excited. I think you're right on with this idea."

"I hope so. But if I'm wrong we'll keep looking. Those coins got into that mud some way. But I really think they're hidden in the walls or ceiling."

They put away their treasure and got read for bed. Trevor slept in the extra bunk and they turned out the light.

"Trev? What if?"

"What if we find it?"

"Yeah, what are we going to do with $3.5 million dollars?"

"I haven't thought about that yet. Let's find it first and then worry about that."

It was a long night for both of them.

THE LOST TREASURE OF BOGUS BLUFF

Chapter 29

The boys arrived at the briar patch carrying the buckets from their last trip up the hill. In addition to their trowels and claw, they added two hammers and two heavy screw drivers. Andy climbed down the rope first and Trevor dropped first one bucket and then the other to him. After Andy backed into the tunnel Trevor climbed down. They met at the split in the tunnels and Trevor led the way down the right one.

"Keep your eyes open for anything that looks out of place," he said over his shoulder.

"I think we should look where we found the coins. If they're hidden like we think, we'll see what to look for. But then we'll have to look at the whole tunnel."

"Yeah, I think that there may be several more places with coins that haven't broken open. We don't want to miss any of them."

They crawled to where they'd cleaned up the mud from the floor and sat down and began looking at the ceiling and walls. Trevor was running his hands over the stone when he stopped and reached for his hammer.

"Look here," he said.

He touched a bump on the top of the wall where the roof of the tunnel met the wall. It was rougher and stuck out a tiny bit.

"I'm going to tap it with the hammer," he said.

Andy watched as Trevor tapped on the spot with his hammer. What looked like solid rock disintegrated as he tapped it. The "rock" was really packed mud and it shattered like glass and fell to the floor.

"Clever," Trevor said. "They chipped a little pocket out of the wall right where it met the roof."

Inside the hole was something black and rough looking. Trevor reached up and pulled on the object and it disintegrated.

"Oh my gosh!" he said as a hail of gold coins rained down on his head.

Andy crawled forward and picked up a handful of the coins.

"Trev, you did it, you found them!"

They were very excited as they picked up coins and dropped them into the first bucket. Trevor reached back up to the hole but it was empty. It had held just one sack of coins. Meanwhile Andy had almost all of the coins collected.

"Let's go out in the sunshine and count them," Andy said smiling widely.

Trevor nodded. "Yeah, let's."

They began crawling back down the tunnel.

"Andy wait," Trevor said.

Andy stopped and Trevor reached down inside his shirt and came up with two coins that had dropped down there when they fell on him. "A couple of stowaways," he said as he dropped them into the bucket.

They crawled as fast as they could to the opening and Trevor crawled through first and then climbed the rope. Andy pushed the bucket in front of him through the tunnel and tied it to the rope so Trevor could pull it up. Then he climbed the rope and they went out of the briar patch and sat down on a big flat stone on the hillside.

They poured the coins out onto the stone and just sat open mouthed looking at the glittering gold. The sun shone on the coins and they sparkled like the day they were minted.

"I can't believe it," Trevor said. "We actually found it."

"When Gramps told us those stories, I figured the odds of the stories being true were maybe 10% and the odds of us finding anything were 0," Andy said.

"Well we sure as heck beat the odds," Trevor said high-fiving Andy.

"Let's count them!"

They began picking up the coins and stacking them in stacks of ten coins. In no time they had little stacks over a large section of the slab of stone. Then Andy began to count the stacks.

"Ninety seven, ninety eight, ninety nine, one hundred... holy smokes, there're a thousand of them," he said.

Trevor nodded. "I figured it would be something like that. They wouldn't just pour them into a bag and not know exactly how many. A thousand coins were 20,000 francs. Each of these coins is 20 francs. I don't know how much a franc was in those days but it must have been pretty worthwhile."

Andy was ciphering in his head. "So if I'm doing this right, this bag is worth about $350,000?"

A grin spread across Trevor's face. He nodded. "This one bag is a small fortune, and there could be how many more bags?"

They both sat there dumbfounded. "Trevor we have to be very careful here and use our heads. This is a life-changing thing."

"You're right. We've got to be very cautious and think things through before we do anything stupid. We can't just go to town and begin to brag about our new found fortune. We have to think this through before we do anything that we'll regret later."

"Ok, so what's next?"

"I think we need to put this batch of coins someplace safe and then go back in and see how many more we find."

"What about the Spanish coins and the American coins?"

Trevor rocked his head back and forth. "You're not happy with three hundred and fifty thousand dollars?"

Andy laughed. "Oh I'm happy, I just wondered if you think the other stories are true too."

"I think finding one story to be true is amazing. I think that two of three would be nearly impossible and three of three... no way. I'd bet the first story evolved into the others as the years went by. You know how it is. I bet every cave in the country has a treasure story associated with it."

Andy nodded. "I thought that too. Just like the fair maiden jumping to her death story. Every cliff in the country has one of those too."

"Well, unless we're both having the same dream, this story is a real one and this pile of gold pretty much convinces me, we're two pretty rich guys," Trevor said.

They put the coins back into the bucket and started down the hill. "We need to get something better to carry them in," Trevor said. "Maybe we can find a pillow case."

When they got back to the jeep they turned around and drove back to town. As they crossed the bridge into town they didn't notice a dark green panel van parked at the end of the bridge. The van pulled out behind them and followed them through town.

Chapter 30

"Where are we going to hide the coins?" Andy asked.

"Your hiding place in your room isn't going to hold all of them. Do you have any other trophies?"

"Are you making fun of my trophy again?"

"No... well yes I might have been. Sorry, do you have any other ideas where we can hide them?"

Andy thought for a minute. "I guess we could just hide them in my sock drawer. Mom leaves my laundry in the basket on my bed and I put it away. That should be ok for a while... at least until we see how many coins there are left up in the cave."

Trevor nodded. "Ok, but eventually we have to find a place that is safer than that. We're talking major money here."

Andy's house was empty so they carried the coins right through the living room to his bedroom where they poured them into a sweat sock and put it into the drawer with the other socks inside.

"I'm starving," Trevor said.

"Let's see what Mom's got to eat," Andy said leading the way to the kitchen.

Andy rummaged through the refrigerator and found some bologna and got some bread and mayo. They made sandwiches and went to sit in the living room to eat.

"Ok, so tomorrow we need to go back up to the cave and see how many more stashes of coins we can find."

Trevor nodded. "Let's take some ice cream buckets and a couple of the big buckets. Then we can carry the ice cream buckets into the cave, fill them and carry them out and dump them into the big one. That'd be easier than pushing that big bucket back and forth."

Andy thought that was a good idea. "My batteries have been in my head lamp for quite a while. Let's go up and get some new ones so we don't have to take the chance of them running out while we're in the cave."

They cleaned up their mess and walked out to the jeep. As they got in the green van drove past them on the street.

Andy turned to Trevor. "Did you see that guy driving that van?"

Trevor shook his head. "I wasn't looking… why?"

"It looked like Voldemort."

"You mean the guy from the coin shop?"

Andy nodded. "Yeah, I'm sure it was the creepy guy from the coin shop."

Trevor looked in his rear view mirror. The van was driving very slowly down the street going away from them. Trevor started the jeep and pulled a U turn and began to follow it. He got up behind it and the van sped up. Trevor sped up behind it and got closer.

"Write down that license number," he said to Andy.

Andy found a slip of paper and an old pen in the glove box and wrote down the license plate number.

"I got it, so what should we do with it?" Andy asked.

"I'm not sure but they always write down the license number on TV. I guess I just got excited."

Andy looked at his friend and shook his head.

The van made several turns and then turned onto a county road that led out of town. When it got to the county road it sped up.

"Should I follow him?" Trevor asked.

"Let him go, I'm not sure it was Voldemort anyway."

"Strange," Trevor said.

Andy nodded. They drove to the hardware store and bought batteries. They both had to work the afternoon shift so they put the batteries in the back of the jeep and went home to rest before their work.

After they were both finished several hours later they went to Trevor's house to sleep. They planned on getting up early to go back to the cave, and since the green van knew where Andy lived, they thought it might be a better idea to sleep at Trevor's house. They pulled his jeep into the garage so it wasn't visible from the street.

They weren't sure if the green van meant anything, but with the amount of money they had hidden, they didn't want to take any chances.

Chapter 31

Trevor's alarm went off at 5 am. He shut if off and rolled over in his bed.

"Andy... time to get up," he said yawning.

"You go first."

Trevor lay there a minute and then sat up on the edge of the bed. He looked over at Andy in the other twin bed. Then he got up, went to the bathroom, showered and when he came back to the bedroom Andy was sitting up scratching his head.

"Tell me again why we have to do this so early?"

Trevor laughed. "So if that *was* Voldemort, we can get out of town without him seeing us."

Andy nodded. "Ok, just wondering." He shuffled off to the bathroom and Trevor went to the kitchen and scrambled some eggs, made some toast and poured each of them a glass of milk. Andy joined him and soon they were finished with breakfast and driving across the bridge on their way to the cave. They went past the local motel and Trevor slowed down.

"Look," he said, "the green van."

Sure enough the green van that they'd seen the previous day was parked at the motel.

"Pull over," Andy said.

Trevor pulled onto the shoulder of the road.

"I'm going to sneak over there and let the air out of a couple of his tires," Andy said.

"What? What if he sees you?"

"It's not even 6 am. He's sleeping and I'm sure the guy who owns the motel is sleeping too."

"But what if it's not him?"

"I'd bet three gold coins it is."

"Ok but be careful."

Andy opened the glove compartment and took the pen out that he'd used the previous day. He unscrewed the pen and removed the top and refill. Then he stuck the lower part of the pen shaft in his pocket. He got out of the jeep and snuck across the road and slipped along the edge of the motel until he was at the van. He squatted down and took the pen from his pocket, took off the valve stem cap and let the air out of the rear left tire and then the right one. Then he snuck back to the road, ran across and got in the jeep.

"There, that'll slow him down a little."

They proceeded up the river and parked where they usually parked. Before they got out, Trevor turned to Andy. "Why don't we park up the road a little way? In case Voldemort is following us, why not throw him off the track a bit?"

Andy grinned. "I like it."

They drove up the road about half a mile and pulled into a turn off below Judith's Point hill. They grabbed their tools and buckets and walked along the road back to Bogus Bluff and then climbed up the hill to the briar patch.

"Ok, let's go back where we found that bag of coins and work all along that wall from back to front. Then we'll see from there," Trevor suggested.

"Sounds like a plan," Andy agreed.

They crawled into the cave carrying one of the ice cream buckets, their hammers and a trowel. Andy stopped about ten feet from the end and began examining the wall and ceiling. Trevor crawled on to the end and started from there.

The bright lights from the LED lamps really made the rock visible. They began running their hands over the rock feeling for anything different. Then if they found something suspicious they'd take their hammer and tap on it. Most times they just tapped on some dirt that had accumulated on the rock.

"Found one!" Andy said excitedly.

Trevor crawled over to his friend. Andy had tapped on a spot and the hammer went right into the mud making a hole. They looked at the hole and saw black canvass behind the dried mud.

"Break it open," Trevor whispered quietly.

Andy tapped on the mud and it dropped away from the little niche. The canvass bag was lying on its side, the string still tied around the end. It was about the size of big hoagie bun. Andy took hold of it carefully and it came out of the hole intact. He turned it in his hand and they could see lettering on the side of the cloth.

"A...M...E...R... American...T... R... American Trading Company," Andy said. He looked up at Trevor, "This is it... this is really the treasure Gramps told us about, Astor's money."

"Holy smokes, just think," Trevor said, "the last time somebody held this it was 200 years ago."

Andy put the bag into the ice cream bucket carefully so it wouldn't fall apart. Then he turned to Trevor.

"Let's keep looking," he said with a huge grin on his face.

Trevor scampered back to where he'd been working and Andy began from that spot on, looking carefully for the telltale signs of yet another bag of gold.

Chapter 32

Trevor found the next bag of coins ten minutes later. The canvass bag was rotted badly and fell apart when he opened the hole. Many of the coins fell out onto the floor but he caught a lot of them with his bucket.

"Some of these niches must have not been airtight," he said. "The canvass bags rotted in the ones where air and moisture got in and stayed intact in the sealed ones."

They kept working on that side of the tunnel until they'd looked at the whole length of it. There were four sacks of coins in their buckets when they got back to the entrance to the tunnel.

"I'm getting hungry," Andy said.

"Yeah, let's quit for today and take this back and count it," Trevor said grinning from ear to ear. "We must have over a million dollars here Andy," he said.

He hefted the bucket. "These are probably 20 or more pounds of gold in each bucket. Just imagine, at about $1,500 per ounce... it's hard to comprehend."

"Jeez, I never thought of that. Holy smokes, at $350,000 per bag we've got nearly two million dollars worth of these coins! What the heck?"

Trevor crawled through the entrance tunnel first and climbed up the rope. Then Andy tied first one and then the other ice cream bucket on the rope and Trevor hauled them up. Then Andy climbed up. Trevor had already dumped the coins into the big bucket, carefully laying the intact bag in the bottom. He picked up the bucket.

"Whoa, this is heavy, I'd say forty pounds at least," he said.

"This is surreal," Andy said shaking his head. "We're talking about pounds of gold. Pounds Trev! I'm afraid I'm going to wake up pretty soon and this will all be a dream."

"It's not a dream, I guarantee it."

They took turns carrying the bucket down the hill. Then they walked along the shoulder of the road back to Trevor's jeep. Two cars passed them but neither took any notice of them. Two teenagers carrying a bucket along the river wasn't anything that seemed out of the ordinary.

"They probably think we've got fish in this," Andy said.

Trevor nodded. "Probably so."

They loaded up and drove back to town. When they got to the motel they saw that both of the tires on the green van were now inflated. Just as they stopped at the stop sign, Voledmort came out of a room and stopped short and stared at them.

"It IS him," Andy said.

"I knew it. That guy at the coin shop sent him out here. He's looking for our gold."

"Yeah I agree, but how would he know about it?" Andy asked.

"I'm sure they know how to use the internet just like we do Andy," Trevor said.

"Oh man, sure, they researched that coin, added the word treasure and bingo... Bogus Bluff."

They continued on into town. Trevor looked in the mirror and Voldemort was following them.

"He's back there again," he said.

"We don't want to go to my house then. If he thinks we might have more coins he'll break in when nobody's home."

"So what do we do?"

"Let's go to Gramp's house."

Trevor nodded. They drove over to Andy's grandpa's house and pulled into the driveway. They watched as Voldemort turned one block early.

Gramps was sitting in his lawn chair with glass of ice tea watching his sprinkler water the garden. The boys walked up and the old man smiled.

"Grab a couple of those lawn chairs and pull up and have a little rest," he said. "Would you like some ice tea?"

"That'd be great Gramps," Andy said.

"Good, fill my glass up when you go inside then too," the old man said handing Andy the nearly empty glass. He winked at Trevor.

Andy took the glass and went inside. Gramps turned to Trevor, "So what have you guys been up to?"

Trevor took a deep breath. "We've been busy, and I don't think you're going to believe what we have to tell you."

Grampa's eyebrows went up. "Oh? Do tell."

"I better wait for Andy, this is a really big deal," Trevor said.

A couple of minutes later Andy came carrying a tray with three glasses of tea on it. He handed the old man his glass and then gave one to Trevor and took one for himself.

"So, what's this big secret you guys have?" Gramps said.

Andy looked at Trevor. "You told him?"

Trevor shook his head. "I told him we have something big to tell but waited for you."

Andy nodded. "Gramps, remember when you told us about the treasure up at Bogus Bluff?"

The old man nodded and grinned. "You went up there again did you?"

"Yeah we did."

"Did you get a lot of exercise climbing around in there?"

Andy nodded, "That we did Gramps. Actually we spent a lot of time up there searching and trying to figure out the secret."

The old man's eyes were twinkling. "You guys know I was just telling you a tall tale don't you? I knew you wouldn't find anything but the fun is in the search isn't it?"

Trevor smiled at the old man. "You're right about that. We had fun crawling around in that cave. Then we sat down and tried to figure out that if... if the story was true, why hadn't someone else found the gold before us. And you know what?"

The old man shook his head.

"Because they were looking for it from the wrong end of the hill... we began looking for the other end of the tunnel, where the lost tunnel started up on the hill."

The old man was looking strange. "And what is it you're telling me?"

"Did you ever wonder why the tunnel with the room in it was so short and why it wasn't like the others" Andy said.

"Well no I guess..."

"We wondered about that and we took a close look at the back end of that tunnel."

"And, what did you find?"

"We found that the end of the tunnel was not real Gramps. There was a slab of stone blocking the tunnel that came from the top of the hill just like the others."

Gramps had a strange look on his face. He turned to Trevor and looked questioningly. Trevor just grinned, having a hard time to keep from blurting out the news.

Andy got up and walked to the jeep, opened the door and lifted the pail out of the back. He carried it with two hands to the edge of the garden and sat it in front of the old man's chair.

"We found this... so far," he said.

The old man's mouth dropped open as he looked down into the pail. He looked up at the boys and a grin spread across his face. "Are these real? They're not the ones filled with chocolate are they?"

The boys shook their heads. "They're not chocolate. Pick up a handful," Trevor said.

Chapter 33

"Oh my Lord, you did it," the old man said. "It really was there and you figured it out."

Andy handed him a handful of coins. "These are worth about $350 each Gramps. We have another bag at home and think there are probably another 5 or 6 bags hidden yet."

"Three hundred and fifty dollars each, there must be hundreds of them in here," the old man gasped.

"This is about $1.4 million and with what we have at home we have about $1.75 million."

The old man looked at them. "Million? Did you say over a million dollars?"

Andy grinned. "Yeah Gramps, I said million. And if we find the rest we'll have about three and a half million... give or take a few hundred thousand."

The old man picked up his tea and took a drink with a shaking hand.

"Are you alright Gramps?" Andy asked.

"I'm just a little stunned. I had no idea that the story was true, and no clue that you two would be clever enough to figure out where the gold was. Is this all? I mean the Spanish and American treasure...have you looked for it too?"

"We haven't looked yet... we just found this the past two days. We've been pretty busy with this treasure, but it's kind of hard to comprehend isn't it?"

Gramps nodded. "I'd say it's hard to comprehend. My 16 year old grandson and his friend are millionaires. Yeah that's a little strange."

"We have you to thank though Gramps," Andy said. "If you hadn't given us the $2 lecture on cave formation we'd have never figured out the secret. I guess no one else wondered why that cave was so different than the other two, or maybe they just didn't have a smart Gramps."

"So you figured it out from my cave lecture?"

"Yeah, when we thought about it, we wondered why the middle cave was so short. Then we figured it out, the real beginning of the cave was way up on the hill someplace like the others. We put those things together and did a lot of climbing and looking and found the entrance, hidden in a sinkhole on top of the hill. From there it was just a matter of figuring out where they'd hidden the sacks of gold," Andy said.

"We've got a problem though," Trevor said.

"What kind of problem?" Gramps asked.

"We found three coins last week and took them to Madison to a coin dealer to see what they were worth. He gave us $900 for the three of them but he made us give him our names and addresses and when we left his worker took down our license plate number. We gave him a fake name, but they must have found out who we really are from my license plate. His helper must have figured out about Astor's gold because we saw the guy here. Yesterday we saw him in town in a green van and he's been following us."

"Are you sure? There are lots of green vans in the country."

"We're sure. This guy looks like Voldemort.'

Grandpa looked quizzical. "Who's Voldemort?"

"From Harry Potter," Andy said.

"Harry who?"

"Oops, generation gap," Andy said, "Harry Potter is a series of books and movies. Voldemort is the bad guy, an evil wizard. He's got a shaved head, thin face that looks like a skull, real pale skin and he dressed in black from head to toe. This guy looks just like him.....and he's lurking around here following us."

"So do you think he might be willing to do you harm to get your treasure?"

"We're not sure. We don't think he knows about the new coins. We just found them. That's why we came here. He knows where I live. He drove by yesterday when we were there. But he doesn't know where Trevor lives. He was following us so we came here to see what you thought we should do."

"Ok, let's think this through," the old man said. "First the gold.....do you plan on telling everyone you found it?"

The boys shrugged.

"I think you should keep it to yourselves. If you turn up with millions of dollars of gold, there are going to be all kinds of legal claims and who knows what will happen. So that means you can't go to the police about this Voldemort fella so we need to take care of him on our own."

"What do you mean take care of him?" Andy asked.

"I mean that we need to make him aware that we will take unkindly to him interfering with your treasure hunting. I'm sure we can come up with a deterrent that will cause him to go back to Madison and leave us alone."

The boys grinned. "That sounds like fun too."

"Ok," the old man said, "now what are we going to do with this pail full of gold?"

"The first bag we found is in my sock drawer," Andy said.

"This is a little much for a sock drawer," Gramps said. "I've got just the place."

He got up and Andy picked up the pail and followed him into the garage. The old man reached up and pulled a cord hanging down from the ceiling and a trap door opened. A set of stairs dropped down.

"Take that bucket up there and put it someplace in plain sight. Set something on it so it looks like an old bucket and no one will ever look at it."

Andy climbed the stairs and did exactly what the old man said. He sat the bucket next to an old ice chest and put a bushel basket full of canning jars on top of it. Then he climbed down and they closed the trap door. Their gold was hidden in plain sight, the safest place.

"Gramps we're going to go up to the cave tomorrow and try to find the rest of the gold. We think we know about where it is. Then we can deal with He-Who-Shall-Not-Be-Named."

"He what?"

"Nevermind."

Chapter 34

Since Voldemort already knew where Andy lived, the boys went to his house to spend the night. Andy checked his sock drawer and the coins were still there safe and sound. They ate and showered and Andy loaned Trevor some clothes since they were the same size.

"Ok, so how do we get out to the cave without Voldemort following us tomorrow?" Andy asked.

"I was thinking about that. What if we call your Gramps and ask him to meet us somewhere and haul us out there? Then he can come back later and pick us up."

Andy nodded. "That's a good idea. How about we drive up to the diner in the morning for breakfast and then sneak out the back way and have Gramps meet us in the back parking lot?"

"Good idea," Trevor said, "and we can get a good breakfast too. I guess we can afford it."

Andy grinned. "I believe we can."

He called his grandpa and they made the plans for the morning. The old man was all for the idea and said he'd be there ready for action. The rest of the afternoon and evening the boys sat in the back yard by the fire pit talking and resting. They saw

Voldemort drive past the house several times.

"He's going to get tired of watching us," Trevor said as the van slowly crept past.

"They made me," Voldemort said into his cell phone.

"What do you mean?"

"Those kids, they saw me and they know I'm watching them."

"I thought you were going to be discreet."

"Have you ever been to this little town? There's about 1,500 people and anyone who hasn't lived here for the last ten years, kind of stands out. They know everyone by first name. Don't worry, I'm still on them. They've been leaving town and sneaking around so I think they're still looking for more coins. I'm going to keep an eye on them and let them do the work. Then I'll just relieve them of their treasure. If they resist, I'll use my powers of persuasion to change their minds."

"You have to be careful. We don't want anything leading back to us."

"I have that all planned. This river here is very treacherous. People drown in it every summer. I think our boys are going to have a terrible accident and by the time they find their bodies, they'll never be able to find the cause of death and rule it drowning. They have signs at every boat landing warning of treacherous currents and undertows."

"Just be sure to be careful and not leave anything behind that points to us, I don't want to spend my remaining years in jail.

"Don't worry I have it all under control."

"Keep me posted."

The boys parked in front of the diner and took a booth that allowed them to keep an eye on the front window but far enough back that it was hard to see them from outside. Gramps came in by the back door and joined them. He had a grin on his face.

"Are we ready for a little sleight-of-hand?" he asked.

"Let's have breakfast first. This treasure hunting is hard work, and we're growing boys and growing boys must eat," Andy said.

Gramps laughed and waved to the waitress. They all ordered and while they were waiting for their food Trevor said, "Don't make it obvious, but look across the street in between the post office and the bank... in the alley."

Andy yawned and stretched and turned his head to look. "What's-His-Name is hiding and watching us," he said giggling.

"Who's his name?"

"Voldemort Gramps," Andy laughed.

"In these movies they're about wizards and witches and this Voldemort guy is an evil wizard who it trying to take over the world. The people think its bad luck to say his name so they call him He-Who-Shall-Not-Be-Named and You-Know-Who through the movie."

Gramps looked at them. "I'm real sorry I missed that one, I'll have to get it on video tape."

"They don't make video tapes anymore Gramps. Now they have DVD's."

"Well I'll have to buy a DVD machine and then watch them," the old man said.

The boys laughed. "I've got all eight of them on DVD, I'll bring them over and you can watch them," Trevor said.

"Eight movies... I'll have to pop a lot of popcorn," the old man said.

Just then their breakfast came and they stopped talking and began eating. When their plates were clean Andy grabbed the check and went up to pay the bill. He came back and Gramps handed him $5 for his share.

"Our treat," Trevor said. "We've recently come into a little money."

"Oh right... I forgot," Gramps said. "Well, shall we go for a ride?"

They snuck out the back door and loaded their empty bucket

into Gramps' car and then the boys slid down in their seats as Gramps drove right past Voldemort. He nodded politely as they went past.

"Handsome fella," he said.

"Yeah if you like skeletons," Andy said peeking up over the seat.

They drove out to the bluff and Gramps let them off.

"I'll come back at about 4 pm?"

"Sounds good… thanks Gramps," Andy said.

They watched the old man turn around and drive away.

"He's pretty cool," Trevor said.

"Yeah, he sure is… well, shall we go and get muddy?"

"We shall."

Chapter 35

They began hiking up the hill with Trevor in the lead. When they were about half way up Trevor stopped short and backed up.

Andy turned and ran back a little way. "Snake?" he asked.

Trevor turned around. "Jeez what a sissy....no come and look."

Andy cautiously moved forward and looked down. "Holy smokes," he said.

There was a trail about an inch wide of red ants scurrying back and forth across the trail. They were the big ants with red front ends and black back ends. There were millions of them.

"Those are fire ants," Trevor said. "They're dangerous. I've seen a video about them and they can kill small animals when they attack. Thousands of them bite and keep biting until they just overwhelm the critter. It's pretty gruesome."

"What do you mean, small animals?"

"Things like squirrels or snakes, I saw a video of them killing a raccoon once."

"Nasty, where are they going?"

Trevor stepped off the trail and followed the stream of ants down the hill.

"There is a dead possum down here. It looks like they're biting little pieces of it off and carrying it back up the hill." He hiked back up the hill and looked to the other side of the trail.

"Here's their nest," he said pointing into the grass a few yards off the trail. "Come and look."

Andy carefully walked through the grass and saw the mound with hundreds of ants crawling over it and the trail of ants leading into a hole near the bottom. It looked like a small version of one of those termite hills you see in movies about Africa.

"Jeez, there must be millions of them," he said.

Trevor nodded. "We'll keep away from them. I've been bitten by them and it hurts like hell."

They carefully walked back to the trail and stepped across the line of ants. When they got to the briar patch they crawled through and climbed down into the cave as they had before. They went all the way back to the end again and started searching the left side of the cave for hidden niches holding bags of coins.

"I'd bet they're going to be in the same area as the others but I'd hate to miss any," Andy said, "so I suppose we better look pretty carefully at all of the area."

Trevor found the first coins. He chipped open a very tightly sealed niche and the sack inside was intact. He carefully removed it and laid it in his bucket. Andy found a second sack that disintegrated when he chipped away the mud and spilled coins all over the floor of the cave. While he was picking them up Trevor found a sack that held together long enough to be laid into his bucket.

"That's another million dollars," he said to Trevor.

Trevor looked up and grinned. "Did you ever think you'd say something like that? Hey Trev. I found another million dollars."

Andy shook his head. "Never in a million years."

The hours passed they found themselves near the front end of the cave and had found no more sacks of coins.

"Well, I guess that's it," Trevor said.

Andy nodded. "So we have eight sacks with 900 to 1,000 coins in each sack. I guess we can live with that."

"So we're talking two and a half million dollars?" Trevor asked.

"Seems like... holy crap that's a lot of money!"

"Let's get out of here," Trevor said.

Andy crawled through the opening first and climbed the

rope. Then Trevor put all the coins into one bucket and tied it to the rope. Andy pulled it up and Trevor climbed up behind the coins. He left the extra bucket lying on the ground and they crawled back out of the briars.

"We've got over an hour until Gramps comes to pick us up, let's go down by the river and wash off and wait there," Trevor suggested.

They hiked down the hill and crossed the ant trail, avoiding disturbing the ants. Then they climbed down over the river bank and took off their shoes and waded into the water rinsing mud off their jeans and washing their hands and faces in the cool water. When they were clean they sat on the grassy river bank and looked into the bucket of coins.

"It's hard to believe how much money this is worth," Andy said.

Trevor nodded. "Such small pieces of metal and worth so much... it kind of blows your mind doesn't it?"

"So, what are we going to do with it?"

"You mean right now?"

"No, I mean now that we have $2.5 million dollars, what the heck are we going to do with it?"

Trevor looked at his friend. "I don't have a clue Andy, but I know we have to think about it very carefully or we could make a choice that would ruin our lives. We need to really think this through."

Just then a vehicle passed on the road above them. It was a green van and it was driving slowly while Voldemort looked out the window and up the hill toward Bogus Bluff.

"It's him!" Andy whispered.

"He must have found something on the internet about Bogus Bluff. He probably found a map to where it is," Trevor said.

"You don't think he might have followed Gramps?"

"Nope, I bet he just got tired of waiting and found out he'd been hoodwinked. Then he either asked someone or found out where this place is."

Chapter 36

Voldemort cruised past going back toward town a few minutes later. He didn't notice the boys sitting in the grass next to the river.

"We've got to do something about him," Andy said.

Trevor nodded. "You're right about that. We have to do something that will make him decide he's better off in Madison or someplace besides here. Maybe Gramps can come up with something."

Gramps drove up about forty five minutes later and the boys climbed up over the bank onto the shoulder of the road. They climbed into the car and Gramps drove down the road a little way, turned around in a driveway and started back toward town.

"So?" he said.

Trevor took the lid off the ice cream bucket and showed him the coins.

"We found three more bags, so that makes eight bags all together."

The old man shook his head. "Which makes the total what?"

"Around eight thousand coins at around $350 each or two and a half million dollars," Andy said.

The old man slowed down and pulled onto the shoulder.

"Two and a half million dollars... amazing."

The boys grinned. "So now we need some advice as to what the heck to do with it?"

Gramps pulled back onto the road. "That's the big question isn't it? You've also got to figure out a way to discourage Mr. Voldemort to go away and leave you alone," he said.

"That too," Trevor said.

They drove back to the old man's house and put the coins up in the attic of the garage with the rest that was already up there. Then they sat in the back yard by the garden.

"Ok, so let's see what we have here," the old man said. "First does anyone have a claim to the money? Second, does the government have a claim? Third does the landowner have a claim? Anything else?"

"Isn't that enough?" Andy said.

Gramps smiled. "Well I doubt the American Fur Company would still have any claim to the money. It's been lost for 200 years and as far as I know the Astor family has nearly as much money as God, so I wouldn't worry about that part. As for the government, I don't know. We'd have to consult a lawyer and that could lead to a nightmare. If the government has a claim you'd have to give them a part of it and you know they way they spend money....they'd waste it on some windmill someplace and it'd be gone. Then you'd have to pay a bunch to the lawyer and that would also be a big waste. The guy who owns the land might be a different story though."

"We thought about that too," Andy said. "We think we should share with him."

"That's a good idea. I know the man and he's not a money-grubber. He's comfortable already so if you guys are ok with it I'll talk to him and see what he says."

The boys agreed.

"Gramps, we've talked about it a little the past few nights when we were laying in our beds talking and we'd like to use some of it to help people. We thought maybe we could give some of it anonymously to people who needed help or organizations that need money."

The old man smiled. "That is a good idea, and I'm happy you think that way. I'd like to see you guys keep enough to make sure you have a college fund and enough to get you started in life."

"Oh we're not going to give it all away, we just thought that it might be a good idea to help out," Trevor said.

"I agree," Gramps said.

"So that leaves old You-Know-Who," Andy said. "Gramps, can you take us out there like we did this morning again tomorrow? We want to sift through the mud in the area where we found the open sacks of coins to get the ones that might have fallen and got buried."

"Eight thousand aren't enough?" the old man said grinning.

"Waste not, want not," Trevor said. "At three hundred dollars each, we're not going to leave any coins behind if we can help it."

"Sure, I'll meet you tomorrow, same time same place. I wish I was a little younger, I'd like to climb up there and see this cave."

"It's a pretty good hike Gramps," Andy said.

"Oh I was just thinking out loud," he said. "You guys are the treasure hunters, I'm just the chauffer."

"I found the cave," Voldemort reported.

"You went inside it?"

"No I found out where it is and drove past. I saw the opening in the front of the hill. It's a long way up and it looks like a hard climb. I might need help."

"Austin is here working in back. He's cleaning up some stuff that came in. He's young and fit, but not too bright."

"I'll check things out and let you know. I might need his help."

"Are those kids still messing around up there?"

"They got away from me today. The one kid's grandpa helped them slip past me

They're clever but I know where they live and I know where

the grandpa lives. I've got a plan that I think will get us every last coin they've found."

"You need to find that gold and get rid of those kids," his partner said from the coin shop in Madison.

"Don't worry, I'm on it. I've asked around and I know where the second kid lives now too. Even if they slip past me tomorrow, I know where they're going."

"Ok, keep me posted. I've put out feelers in the coin industry and there's a huge interest in those coins. Coins like that that never got into circulation are worth a fortune. This could be our ticket to retirement."

"I'll call you tomorrow."

Chapter 37

G ramps had his morning coffee shortly after 6 am. There hadn't been any rain for several days so he went out to the garden and turned on the hose and sat in his lawn chair and watered the vegetables while he drank his coffee. The garden was looking good, he thought. If the boys got finished with their treasure hunting he'd have to get them back over for another weeding session soon though.

"I sure got the surprise of my life when those boys actually found that gold," he thought to himself. "They're a lot cleverer than I thought they were."

He heard a sound behind him and turned to look.

"Don't move a muscle," a voice said from behind him.

"What the? Who the hell are you?" Gramps said turning. When he saw the man the boys had been calling Voldemort his heart beat a little faster.

"What do you want here?" he said.

"I told you not to move."

"Yeah, well that's your problem. You're standing on my land, so don't get so pushy Mr."

The man stepped up right behind him. "I want you to get up and come with me. Step into the garage and get into the van I have parked by the outside door. If you make a sound or call out, I'll have to go in the house and deal with your wife... and I don't think you'd like what I'd do to her."

"Leave my wife out of this," Gramps said. "My wallet is on the kitchen counter I'll get it and give you all my money."

"I don't want your money old man, I need you to come with me and if you give me any trouble I'll put a bullet into you and then come back and do the same to your wife."

"I'll come with you. I don't know why you'd want a sick old

man like me but I won't give you any trouble."

He got up and sat his half empty coffee cup on the lawn chair and Voldemort stepped behind him and shoved a pistol into his back.

"Just move and get into the car," he said.

Gramps walked through the garage and out the open door and there was the green van sitting in the driveway. Voldemort motioned for him to get in the side door. When he was inside, Voldemort snapped a handcuff on his wrist and motioned for him to sit on the floor. Then he snapped the other end of the handcuff to an eye bolt that was welded to the frame of the van. When Gramps was secured Voldemort got in the driver side and locked the doors.

"Keep your mouth shut and everything will be just fine. If you make noise I'll have no choice but to shoot you. Now we're going for a little drive and we're going to talk about that grandson of yours and his friend and that gold they've found."

"What the hell are you talking about?" Gramps said. "Are you drunk Mister?"

Voldemort laughed. "Don't act all old and senile with me old man. I know those boys have been over here talking to you and yesterday you helped them lose me and took them out to the cave. I'm not as stupid as you think. I can do research on the internet just like those boys did. I've seen three of the coins, so I know they found the treasure."

"They found three coins you dope!"

"So why have they been up there every day since looking for more?"

"They've been looking but they didn't find anything. Why do you think they'd keep going up there if they had found any more coins? They got lucky and found three coins. God only knows how they got there but that's all they found. The rest of those coins are long gone Mister, long gone, if they were ever really there."

Voldemort looked over at the old man. "Well you old fart

we're going to find out aren't we?"

"Right now I'm going to deliver a message to those boys and then you and I are taking a little drive."

The alarm clock went off and Andy reached over and shut it down.

"Jeez that thing is loud," he complained.

"You seem not to grasp the concept of an alarm clock. If it played a lullaby you'd just keep right on sleeping." Trevor said grinning.

Andy gave him a sour look.

"Jeez you're not a morning person are you?" Trevor said laughing.

They got up and took turns in the shower, dressed and walked out to Trevor's jeep. When they got in they noticed something on the windshield under the wiper. Andy got back out and pulled a sheet of paper out from under the blade. He opened it and turned white.

"Oh no... he's got Gramps," he said handing the paper to Trevor.

Trevor opened the paper and read what was on it:

I HAVE THE OLD MAN. WILL CALL WITH INSTRUCTIONS.

"How would he know my number? Andy asked.

"If he has your grandpa he probably got it from him."

"Trev, what are we gonna do?" Andy asked.

"Just let me think a minute," Trevor said.

Chapter 38

"Capitol Gold and Coin Shop," the owner of the shop said as he picked up the phone.

"I snatched the old man," Voldemort reported.

"You did what? Do you mean the grandpa?"

"Yeah, those kids will cough up the gold if I have the old man. Then I just let him go and we're on our way to Tahiti."

"They know who you are, and I'd bet the old man does too. How are we going to get away if they lead the cops right to us?"

There was silence for a minute. "Well then they'll all have a terrible accident. It doesn't matter to me."

"Oh man, this is getting out of control. I didn't plan on anything like this when I sent you out there."

"Well, we're still ok. Nobody will have a clue what's going on. Those three coins the kids brought to you are the only ones they've spent I bet. They've been hunting for the rest ever since

DAN BOMKAMP

I've been here. I think once they've found them they'll start to worry about selling them."

"You better hope so," the man said.

"I need some help. I'm in Spring Green at a little motel. I brought the old man here in my van but the kids know the van so when I got the room yesterday and rented a car. I need somebody to baby sit the old man while I go and get the gold from those boys."

"I don't have much help around right now. The only one here is Austin."

"Austin.....he's about as dumb as they come. Do you think he can keep an old man from getting loose?"

"He's all I've got. He'll keep his mouth shut and we don't have to pay him much."

"Ok, send him out. Have him meet me at the Old Towne Motor Court, room 26."

"He'll be there in a couple of hours."

"Ok, don't worry I have this all under control."

"Yeah, you better," his boss said.

Voldemort was out in the parking lot when he phoned and he walked back into the room where Gramps was handcuffed to the bed. His right arm was locked to the upper end of the frame but his left arm was free.

"As pale as you are, prison will work out just fine for you," the old man said.

Voldemort grinned. "You've got a smart mouth on you old man."

Gramps just smiled. "It doesn't take much to one-up present company."

"I have a baby sitter coming to keep you entertained. Then when he gets here I'm going to contact that grandson of yours and let him know that we'll trade you for the gold."

Gramps shook his head. "You're going to be disappointed. I'm worth about three bucks and that's not much for the time in prison you'll get for kidnapping."

156

"We'll see won't we?" Voldemort replied.

"When is lunch being served? You interrupted my morning coffee and I didn't get my eggs and toast since you made me leave with you. At least you can feed me."

"There's a diner down the street. I'll get you something but I have to gag you and tie your free hand to the bed frame."

"Oh you can let me without the gag, I promise I won't yell."

Voldemort laughed and picked up the gag from the second bed. "Open," he said.

"I think we should call the cops," Andy said.

"What do we tell them? We found two and a half million dollars worth of 200 year old gold and a walking skeleton kidnapped your grandpa to get it from us?"

"Ok, I see what you mean it does sound a little crazy. But what can we do?"

"Voldemort wants the gold. But he must realize that we know who he is and where he works, so obviously he won't leave us around if we give it to him."

"You mean he'd kill us?"

"Andy, we're talking about a fortune in gold. There are people who'd kill for a six pack of beer."

"So what do we do?"

"I'm working on it. Let's see what his demand is when he calls."

Chapter 39

Voledmort came back carrying a sack and a paper carrying box with two cups of coffee. He took the gag from Gramps mouth untied his hand and handed him a sandwich. Gramps held it in his right hand while he un-wrapped it and then transferred it to his left hand so he could eat.

"Mmm, not bad, I like egg salad," he said. "You won't like me in an hour or so though."

"I'm not going to be here in an hour, so fart all you like. The kid that's coming to keep an eye on you is dumb as a post so he probably won't even notice."

"Not the sharpest tack in the box?"

Voldemort just grinned. "Not really. But I think he's smart enough to keep an old coot like you under wraps."

He finished his sandwich and dialed Andy's phone number. Andy answered on the first ring.

"Bring the gold to the parking lot at the end of the bridge in an hour," he said into the phone.

"We don't have it with us. We hid it up at the cave. It'll take at least an hour and a half to hike up there and get it."

"Bullshit, I don't believe you."

"Well it's the truth," Andy lied. "We didn't know what to do with it and decided since it'd been safe there for 200 years it would be the best place to keep it."

Voldemort thought for a minute. "How much gold are we talking?"

"We found the whole bag, there are about 900 coins."

"Nine hundred? That can't be all there are. I don't believe

you."

"Well again, I'll tell you, we found one bag so far with 900 coins. You know, that's over $300,000. That would have bought a kingdom in the 1800's. We just found that the other day. You interrupted our search. There might be more but we haven't found it yet."

"Ok, let me think a minute."

Andy covered the phone. "I think he bought it."

"Tell him he has to meet me at the cave and I'll show him where the gold is. Remember you have to tell him your grandma is in the hospital over him grabbing your grandpa and you have to stay with her."

"Ok, I want to see where you found the gold," Voldemort said.

"Ok, Trevor will meet you up at the road by the cave. I can't leave. My granny has had a heart attack or something. When she found out Gramps was missing she had some kind of attack. Please, don't tell Gramps. He has a bad heart and he might do the same. You better hope she doesn't die or I'll hunt you down you freak!"

"Tough shit... you don't scare me kid."

"I want to talk to my grandpa."

"No way. He's fine."

"If I don't talk to Gramps, the deal is off. He could be dead already for all I know."

This was getting out of hand. "Ok but no tricks," Voldemort said.

Andy covered the speaker on his phone and said to Trevor, "Grab a piece of paper and a pen."

Then he put the phone on speaker and said, "Gramps?"

"Andy?"

"Hi Gramps, are you okay?"

"I'm fine. Mr. What's-His-Name just gave me a sandwich. He's a prince."

Andy grinned. "Are you giving him a hard time?"

"You know me Andy. I've been giving people a hard time

since I was born. The world changed in 1926. I've lived in this old town all my life and I intend to live a few more years after this."

Andy frowned. "Uh ok, we're going to cooperate with him."

"That's good. The gold isn't worth anyone's life. Oh hey, if you get time, will you turn on the sprinkler on the garden? It's been so nice this spring, so green, I don't want it go get dry. I was about to do it this morning when Mr. What's His Face interrupted me."

Andy nodded. "Ok, I'll see to it. See you in a while."

Gramps handed the phone back to Voldemort.

"Ok, so no tricks. I have a hardened criminal coming to watch this old fart and all I have to do is call and it's the end for him."

"Don't do anything hasty. We'll cooperate. My Grandpa is worth more than a bunch of gold coins."

"Ok, I'll meet the other kid up there in about an hour."

Voldemort shut the phone and turned to Gramps. "That grandson of yours is smart enough to know he's been bested."

Gramps grinned. "He's a smart boy. I expect he'll do just as he's been told."

Chapter 40

"Well?" Trevor said.

Andy grinned and shook his head. "I think Gramps told us where he is."

Trevor looked confused. "Ok, how did he do that?"

"Read back what he said at first."

"I've been giving people a hard time since I was born in 1926."

"Right... Gramps was born in 1936. He gave us the wrong year. Then he said something about living in this old town all his life. He was born in Minnesota and lived there most of his life. When my mom married and came here, he and my grandma decided to move to be close to her. So he hasn't lived in this old town."

"So he gave us a clue of the number 26 and this old town," Trevor said.

"That's right, let's break it down," Andy said. "What would 26 mean?"

"It could be a highway or... an address?"

"I think an address is more like it but what kind of address is a number like 26?"

"A room number in a hotel or motel!" Trevor said.

"That's got to be it, he's in a hotel or motel in room 26 someplace around here."

"Sure, that has to be it... but where?"

"Read back what he said at the end."

"He said to be sure to turn on the sprinkler on the garden."

"But he said something about it being green."

"He said it's been so green all spring... green all spring, Trev, he's in Spring Green, that's got to be where he is. It makes sense. Voldemort wouldn't take him a long way away or he'd have to drive a long time to get back here. Spring Green is far enough to be safe but not so far away."

"Ok but which motel, there are several of them."

"We could go and look but I think he gave us a clue. He said he's lived in this old town. But he *didn't* live here in this old town."

"I bet if we look up motels in Spring Green there's one called the Old Town Inn or Old Town Motel."

Trevor Googled Spring Green motels and sure enough there was one called the Old Town Motor Court."

Andy nodded. "He's pretty clever. Ok, so you better get up to the cave and get things ready and I'll go to Spring Green and get Gramps."

Trevor jumped in his jeep and took off on the road north and Andy headed east to Spring Green.

When Trevor got to the cave he parked his jeep on the shoulder. The gold they'd found first that was in a sweat sock was lying on the seat next to him. He grabbed it and one of the ice cream buckets and lids and one of the little trowels and started off up the hill. He had to hurry to get everything ready.

He stopped on the trail where the ant trail had been the previous day. Apparently the ants had gotten all they wanted from the opossum because they weren't marching across the trail. He walked into the grass and found the ant mound. It was alive with ants coming and going from all around him. He took the lid off the ice cream bucket and sat it down next to the mound. Then he took the trowel and scooped a chunk of the mound into the pail. The mound came alive with ants spilling out of it by the thousand. He grabbed the lid and snapped it on top of the bucket, along with hundreds of ants and picked up his trowel and sprinted to the trail a few feet away.

The outside of the bucket had hundreds of ants on it and they were climbing up his arm and began biting him. He dropped the bucket and began to wipe ants from his body. They were all over him and biting like mad. It took several minutes to get them off him and then he banged the bucket on the ground to knock off the extra riders on the outside and moved up the trail.

He hadn't gone a few feet when he felt a hot flash of pain on the inside of his thigh. He dropped his pants and pinched an ant off his thigh and tossed its squashed body into the grass. Then he inspected himself more closely finding two more ants on his legs. He took off his shirt and found another ant inside it. He shook off the shirt and put it back on.

Satisfied that he wasn't carrying anymore of the little monsters he made his way the rest of the way up the hill. He carefully made his way into the middle of the briars.

"Ok, Voldemort, you're going to earn your money if you plan to take it from us."

He dropped the sweat sock of coins to the bottom of the hole below the slab of rock and then climbed down and backed into the cave. He took the coins and shinnied down the left tunnel and left them about ten yards into the tunnel. Then he shinnied back out and climbed back up to the top. He took the bucket of ants and hid them in the briars and hurried down the hill to wait for Voldemort in his jeep.

Chapter 41

"The guy who's coming to watch you is unstable, so don't mess with him. I'm not sure if I should even let him alone with you," Voldemort said.

Gramps tried to stifle a grin. "He's a hardened killer?"

"Don't laugh he won't take any crap from you old man."

"I'll try to be on my best behavior," Gramps said.

They waited silently for another three quarters of an hour and then a car with a very loud muffler pulled up outside the room. Voldemort peeked through the side of the curtain. He went to the door and slid the chain back and opened it. A kid who looked to be about 19 walked into the room.

The kid was well over six feet tall, probably about six feet four or five inches and weighed about 130 pounds. He had a Mohawk haircut and three rings in each ear and one in his eyebrow. His arms were tattooed up as far as they were visible. He was wearing a tee shirt with the sleeves cut off and baggy cargo shorts with flip flops on his feet.

"Oh yeah, a hardened criminal," Gramps said grinning at

Voldemort.

"What'd he say?" the kid asked.

"Nothing....you got a gun?"

The kid patted his left pocket. "I got my little 380 special. I'll make a hole big enough in that old man if he screws with me, don't worry."

"Don't be making holes in anyone," Voldemort said. "Just keep him here until I get back... and keep him quiet."

"No prob."

Voldemort looked at the old man and shook his head. "It's hard to get good help." He walked out the door.

Austin grabbed a wooden chair and turned it around so he was resting his arms on the back. "So old man, what shall we talk about?"

"Oh we could talk about how popular you'll be when you get to the penitentiary. I'm sure those big guys there will take special interest in a skinny kid like you. You'll be worth a whole pack of cigarettes I'd think."

"What're you talking about?"

"I'm talking about when you and that walking skeleton you call your boss are arrested and imprisoned for kidnapping."

"We ain't gonna get caught, we got it all planned."

Gramps grinned. "Well that's a load off my mind. I was worrying about what a kid like you would do and here you got it all planned. Silly me."

"Yeah, silly you."

"You might get lucky and get into a segregated part of the prison. It'd be a crime to let a young boy like you put into the general population with all those sex crazed guys. Some of them would kill to get a boy like you... well, let's say to be pals with you."

Austin looked worried. "That's bull, they don't do that stuff."

"I bet you'll command top price. They'll pass you around like a party favor and if you don't perform up to their standards they'll beat you like a Pin'ata'."

"Shut the hell up!"

Voldemort stopped at a gas station and bought a glove-compartment rechargeable flashlight. In case he had to actually go into the cave he wanted to have his own light. He drove along excited at the prospect of getting his hands on 900 of the gold coins he'd seen at the coin shop.

"Those kids are lying about how many other coins there are, but once I get to the cave, I'll either find them myself or torture them until they show me where the rest are."

Half an hour later he saw Trevor sitting in his jeep and he pulled off the road across from him. "You ready to show me the gold?" he asked.

"This isn't fair," Trevor said. "We worked hard to find this gold you don't have any right to it."

Voldemort held up a silver pistol. "This 9mm says I have all the rights in the world."

Trevor nodded. "Ok, let's go."

They got out and Trevor led the way up the hill. Voldemort kept the gun pointed at Trevor's back.

"Keep an eye where you're putting your feet," Trevor said over his shoulder. "There are rattlesnakes up here and I'd hate to see you get bit."

Voldemort laughed. "I bet you would you snot."

They got to the briar patch and Trevor bent low and crawled in. Voldemort didn't get low enough and took a big nasty branch right across the bridge of his nose, ripping a gash that bled like a stuck pig.

Voldemort took a black handkerchief from his pocket and dabbed at it.

Trevor tried to stifle a smile. "Nice hanky, you got on black underwear on too?"

"Shut up and show me the gold," Voldemort growled.

Trevor pointed down the hole. "It's down there."

"What? Why didn't you bring it up?"

"You said you wanted to see where we found it. This is where we found it and where we hid it."

"How do you get in there?"

"You have to go down the rope and then back into that tunnel. It's only about ten feet long and then it opens up and gets larger. The gold is in the left tunnel."

Voldemort stood there thinking.

"I'll go down first," Trevor said.

"Oh sure, I let you go first and then when I back out of that tunnel you bash my head in with a big rock. I'm not that stupid."

"Suit yourself," Trevor said and he stepped back from the hole. "All I know is that Andy is praying that his Grandma doesn't die and he told me to let you have the gold so his Gramps is safe. He doesn't want to lose both his grandparents over a sack of gold."

Voldemort looked down the hole and then looked back at Trevor. "I'm going down," he said.

DAN BOMKAMP

Chapter 42

Andy pulled into the parking lot of the Old Town Motor Court and parked next to the end of the unit. There were 7 cars in the lot and one stood out. In front of room 26 there was a blue Fort Pinto with a red front fender and one window covered with plastic wrap and duct tape. Parked next to it was Voldemort's green van.

"Well, at least he drives a classy car," Andy thought to himself. He sat and thought for a minute and then snuck along the wall and up to the window at room 26.

"Maybe you'll get lucky and find someone you can really get comfortable with and then you can set up housekeeping." It was his Gramps voice.

"Shut the hell up... jeez."

"Those cells are cozy.....I think they're six by ten or something like that. It could be real nice if you get the right roommate."

Andy grinned. Obviously Gramps was giving his guard a hard time. He snuck back to his car and backed out and drove toward a gas station down the road. He went inside and looked over the food offerings and found just what he wanted.

"I'll take a medium pepperoni," he said to the girl behind the counter.

Fifteen minutes later he parked a few doors down from room 26 and got out carrying the pizza box. He put a baseball cap on backwards and walked up to the room door and knocked.

"Pizza!" he said loudly.

There was the sound of someone coming to the door. "What da ya want?"

"I've got your pizza."

"We didn't order a pizza."

"Somebody did. We've been really busy and it was ordered about 45 minutes ago. It just got done."

The door lock clicked and someone opened it enough to look out.

A kid with a Mohawk peeked through the opening. "Is it paid for?"

Andy nodded, "Guy paid with a credit card."

The Mohawk kid grinned. "Well, Marvin must have forgotten to tell me."

He shut the door to take the chain off the lock and when he began to open it again Andy slammed into the door with a block like a lineman and the door flew open. The door slammed into the Mohawk kid's head. The kid yelled, "Hey!" and fell backward onto the floor.

Andy threw the pizza on the bed and jumped on the kid and rolled him over putting a double Nelson on him. He and Trevor had wrestled many times and it was a move Trevor had taught him.

"Hey, what the hell you doing?" the kid yelled.

Andy tightened his grip on him and said, "I'm here to get my Grandpa and if you give me any trouble I'll break both of your shoulders."

Andy heard a cackling laugh and looked up to see his

Grandpa sitting on the bed laughing. "Andy, this young man is Austin, he's my baby sitter."

Andy grinned up at his Grandpa. "Are you ok?"

The old man nodded. "I'm right as rain. Your friend He-Who-Whatever is on his way to get your gold."

"Trevor's waiting for him. He's got a surprise ready. Are you sure you're ok? Do you want me to take you to the doctor?"

"Oh no, no, I'm fine. Actually Mr. Whosis was quite accommodating to me. He got me an egg salad sandwich."

The old man leaned off to the right and there came a muffled sound from the bed.

Andy looked questioningly at his grandpa. "Did you just fart?"

The old man grinned, "Oops slipped. You know how we old folks are... can't hold our farts. It must be all the excitement and the egg salad."

"Oh man! Get me up off the floor, that's nasty!" Austin whined.

Andy and his Gramps laughed till they had tears running down their faces.

Up on the hill at Bogus Bluff Voldemort was straining to get to the bottom of the shaft by sliding down the rope. He made it to the bottom and looked up. Then he got down and stuck his feet into the tunnel and slowly backed out of sight.

Trevor's phone vibrated. He looked at the screen. "HAVE GRAMPS."

Trevor grinned. He crawled over into the briars and retrieved the pail containing the angry ants. He held it up and looked inside. There must have been a thousand of them and they were scurrying around like crazy.

"Hey kid, how far down that narrow shaft is the gold?" Voldemort's voice came up from the hole.

"It's about ten feet. Just watch you'll see it."

He waited at the edge of the hole and listened. He could hear

170

Voldemort cussing and eventually he heard him. "Ok I got it."

"That's it, take it and leave us alone," Trevor said.

"I don't think so kid. We've still got the old man. I'm going to need you and your buddy to come back down here while I observe and we're going to take this cave apart and find the rest of the gold."

"There is no more gold Mister."

"You let me be the judge of that boy."

"Ok, whatever you say," Trevor said quietly.

He waited until he could hear Voldemort crawling in the entrance tunnel. As soon as he saw his bald head appear in the hole, he took the lid off the pail of ants and dumped them. He rapped the bucket on the side of the hole to get them all out.

"What? What the hell are you doing?" Voldemort yelled as ants rained down onto his head.

Then he began to scream.

Chapter 43

"He's got the key in his right pocket," Gramps said to Andy.

Andy applied a little more pressure to his full Nelson and the kid began to squeal. "I'll get it for you, please let me loose."

Andy let off and the kid reached into his pocket and took the key out and handed it over. Gramps held up his wrist and Andy unlocked the handcuff.

"He claims he's got a pistol in his other pocket," Gramps said.

Andy patted the kid's pockets and found the gun. He took it from his pocket and pointed it at him.

"Get up on the bed," he said.

The kid sat on the edge of the bed and Gramps clamped the handcuff onto his wrist.

Austin looked at Gramps. "You must be dead inside old man."

Gramps laughed. "I wish I had more time to spend here, I'd give you a real show."

Andy looked at the little silver gun. "A Saturday night special," he said. "What did you say when I told you the pizza was paid for?"

"What? I don't know. I said Marvin had paid for it I think."

Andy looked at his grandpa grinning. "Do you know what Voldemort's real name is Gramps?"

The old man shook his head but he was grinning, expecting a good laugh.

"It's Marvin Gardens."

Gramps broke out laughing. "That's one of my favorite properties, next to Go to Jail."

Andy and Gramps laughed like mad and Austin just sat there

looking stupid.

"What's so funny" he asked.

"Marvin Gardens, like in the Monopoly game," Andy said.

"What game?"

Gramps shook his head. "I suppose he's one of those Pac Man players," he said.

Andy laughed. "It's Playstation now Gramps but you're probably right."

"Well, let's go and see how Trevor did," Andy said.

"What about me? You can't leave me here," Austin said.

"Why not? What do we owe you?" Andy asked.

"Well, I was good to the old man, I didn't hurt him."

"He was a prince," Gramps said. "I say just shoot him in the knee or something... maybe in the crotch, don't kill him."

"What!? Hey hold on mister, I'm just doing a job!"

Andy laughed. "Don't worry Austin, you're not worth shooting. We are going to leave you here though. If you're lucky your pal Voldemort will come back and get you on his way back to Madison. If not you'll have to raise a ruckus and have the manager call the cops."

"Who's gonna come and get me?"

"Your pal Marvin, the guy who looks like Voldemort."

Austin laughed. "Dude you're right, he does look like Voldemort. I never thought of it before but you're right."

"Gramps are you ready to go?" Andy asked.

"I'm ready, have a nice day Austin."

"Hey, wait a minute. Were you serious about prison? I mean you were just joking about what they do to young guys weren't you?"

"I wasn't joking Austin. You want to do everything you can to stay out of prison. If you get through this little stupid trick without going into the joint, I'd find a new employer and a new line of work. Otherwise, your future is going will not be pleasant."

"Ok, I get it," Austin said.

Gramps opened the pizza box and looked at Austin. "We could leave this for him," he said to Andy.

"Or not, I haven't had lunch yet," he said.

Gramps shook his head. "Dang tough luck Austin... well, take care of yourself. Remember you can stay out of prison if you clean up your act."

Andy took two slices out and then sat the rest of the pizza on the floor, just out of reach of Austin. And they walked out and closed the door.

Voldemort was screaming and slapping ants when Trevor kicked out the rocks holding up the slab. Then he went to the backside of it and worked the come-along until the big rock was just inches from being down flat on the hole.

"Wait! Wait! Please, don't do that!" Voldemort screamed.

"Sorry mister, if I let you back out of there you'll hound us to the day we die. This way no one will ever find you and we'll be safe."

"No! Wait! I promise, I'll go back to Madison and you'll never see me again, please let me out of here these ants are eating me alive!"

"I'll lower the rope a few feet. Tie the gold onto it and your gun."

"What? My gun? I'm not giving you my gun!"

"Ok, goodbye."

"No, no wait! Lower it, hurry up these ants are killing me."

Trevor reversed the come-along and raised the slab back up. Then he lowered the rope so Voldemort could just get a hold of it. He stayed back away from the edge of the hole in case Voldemort tried to take a shot at him. Voldemort slid the rope through the trigger guard and then tied the sock of gold onto the end of the rope. Trevor pulled them up.

Voldemort had his shirt off slapping ants. He was covered with angry red welts and looked pretty darn miserable.

"Get me out of here... please."

"I'm not kidding mister. If we ever see your face around here again, we'll do something to you that will make this look like a Sunday picnic."

"Don't worry I'll never come near you again, let me out, please, please."

Trevor tossed the rope down to him and stood back holding the gun on him as he climbed up to the top. He was covered in welts that looked like nasty pimples with white heads. There must have been a thousand of them on his body.

"I'd go and jump in the river and wash the rest of those ants off if I were you," Trevor said.

Voldemort bulled his way out of the briar patch. He stopped and turned. "You're good kid. But I made a promise and I'll keep it. No amount of gold is worth screwing around with you kids again."

He turned and began running down the hill following the path. Trevor watched him and when he got to the road he ran across it and disappeared over the river bank. Trevor grinned and began walking down to his jeep.

His phone buzzed and he looked at the text. "GOT GRAMPS ALL IS GOOD."

He saw Voldemort getting into his rented car. "Hey you better stop and get your pal in Spring Green. He didn't do very well guarding a 76 year old man."

Voldemort shook his head. "I'm getting a new job. This one isn't worth it." And he drove away.

Chapter 44

When Trevor pulled off the street at Gramps' house he and Andy were sitting in the back yard drinking ice tea. Trevor walked up with a huge grin on his face.

"Well, I think we've seen the last of old Voldemort," he said.

"You convinced him that his best interest was not in being around this vicinity?" Gramps asked.

"Me and ten thousand fire ants convinced him," Trevor said.

"Ouch, that must have been pretty hard on the poor devil."

"Oh he was hurting. He took off his shirt and from what I could see his body and face had hundreds of welts on them. He's going to be feeling pretty sick for a while. But when I lowered the slab of rock and threatened to leave him in the cave for all eternity, he really changed his attitude."

Andy laughed. "That'd do it."

"He promised never to come near us again, and I think he was scared enough that he'll keep that promise."

"Well, good riddance to bad garbage, "Gramps said.

"So now that we're rid of him, what's our next move?" Andy asked.

Gramps spoke up. "You know how I feel about telling everyone about the gold. I think it would become a nightmare and frankly I think you guys would regret the day you found it. I think you should hide it in a safe place, and spend it a little at a time and do good things with it."

The boys nodded. "We've talked about that and that's how we think too."

"What should we do about the guy who owns Bogus Bluff?" Andy asked.

"I'll call him and you guys go and talk to him. I think he'll be very reasonable. As I said he's comfortable money-wise and I don't think he'd be greedy. I do think you should share it with him though," Gramps said.

"We feel that way too. How about you set it up and we'll go and see him?" Trevor said.

Austin was miserable. At first he'd done everything he could to get the handcuff off but to no avail. Then he got hungry. He kicked off his flip flop and could just barely get his toes on the edge of the pizza box. He dragged the pizza over to the bed with his foot and ate the whole thing. That made him thirsty and he had no way to get a drink so the longer he sat there the thirstier he got. Then he had to pee. He was getting to the point where he was about to make a ruckus so the motel manager would come to see what was going on. He thought about dialing 911 but he didn't know how to explain the handcuff. Then he heard a car door slam.

Voldemort opened the door and walked into the room. He was shirtless and covered with nasty red pimples. He stood there and glared at Austin.

"You couldn't even keep an old man from getting away?" Voldemort asked.

"His grandson fooled me. He said he was a pizza man."

"Did you order a pizza?"

"Well, no but he said you did, and... what the hell happened to you?"

"I got bitten by about a thousand red ants, got sealed into a cave and pretty much bested by a 16 year old kid. Kind of like what happened to you without the ants."

"Wow... that must be uncomfortable."

"You have no idea. But I did managed to come away with something that will make it worthwhile," he said. Then he reached into his pants pockets and pulled his hands out and dumped two handfuls of gold coins on the bed."

"I put these in my pockets just in case the kid tried to double cross me, and I guess it was a good idea."

"Holy crap, how much are these worth?" Austin exclaimed picking up some coins with his free hand.

"They're worth about $350 each."

"Each? Wow, we're rich!"

Voldemort grinned. "We?"

"You are going to cut me in aren't you?"

Voldemort nodded. "I'm getting out of the Coin Shop. There's enough here to go someplace and start over. I'll cut you in but you've got to keep your mouth shut."

"I'll go with you. I hate working for that stingy butthead anyway. Let's go someplace warm in the winter and we can start our own coin business. You know enough about it to run a legitimate business. I want to go straight and stay out of jail that's for sure."

Voldemort nodded. "Ok, that's a good plan. Now I have to get a hacksaw and cut you loose, and then we're outa here."

"Cool, but can you bring me that ice bucket first, I gotta pee like a racehorse."

Chapter 45

"That sneaky Voldemort, he stole some of our coins," Trevor said as he finished counting the coins they'd stored in the sweat sock. "He must have stuffed some into his pockets. I count 784 and I think we had almost 900 when we counted them the first time."

Andy grinned. "Well for what he went through I guess we can let him have a few. I know he asked for it but we've got so much more, if this keeps him away from us, it's worth it."

"That's around $44,000 worth of coins," he said. Then he shook his head like he was trying to get water out of his ear. "Do you hear us? We're talking about 44 thousand dollars like it was chump change."

Andy shrugged. "Well, compared to what we have in that pail, it IS chump change."

They'd carried the pail that had been stashed in his grandpa's garage down from the rafters and taken it to Andy's house. With all of the coins in it the thing was more than one person could carry. They decided to see just how many coins they really had before they went to see the man who owned the land the cave was on.

"Ok, let's put them in piles of 100," Trevor said.

So they dumped a pile of coins on the middle of the pool table in the basement and sat on stools from the bar and began counting and piling up coins. After an hour Andy went upstairs and made some sandwiches and then they ate and continued piling up coins.

"I had no idea there'd be so many," Trevor said piling yet another 100 coins up.

They piled coins for nearly two hours and at the end they had

56 leftovers. Then Andy began counting piles silently.

He got done and wrote a number on a piece of paper, added the 56 leftovers in and looked up at Trevor.

"Guess how many."

"Seventy five hundred," Trevor said.

"Close 7,256," Andy said.

"Holy smokes, and if they're worth even $300 each that's....."

"Two million one hundred and sixty thousand," Andy said looking up from his calculator.

"Two million... holy moley Andy," Trevor said.

"And if they're worth $350, which I think is very possible, it jumps up to a little more than two and a half million."

They sat there stunned looking at the piles and piles of glittering gold coins.

"We've got to be real smart about this," Andy said. "This is life-changing money."

Trevor nodded. "You're right about that. Holy smokes, who'd of ever thought?"

"If we just sold it for the price of gold it's more than 14,000 ounces of gold or a little over 90 pounds."

"Wow, I repeat, wow."

"Ok, so where do we put it now?"

"You got some extra sweat socks?" Trevor asked.

Andy laughed, "Not that many but I think we can afford a few pair."

They ended up dividing the coins up into four old pillow cases Andy found in the linen closet. Then they took 3 of them and wrapped the pillow cases in newspaper followed by freezer wrapping paper and put them in the freezer with 'VENISON STEAK' written on the packages.

"That should keep them safe," Trevor said.

"You can count on it. My mom won't cook venison so we don't have to worry about her bothering them. They're just fine there until we can figure something else out."

"Ok, well, let's go see our landowner friend."

Chapter 46

T he boys turned off the county road onto a driveway with a mailbox bearing the name Stadish. That was where the man who owned Bogus Bluff lived according to Andy's grandpa. The old man had called his friend and he was expecting the boys.

"Whoa," Andy said as they crested the hill and saw the house. "That's a beautiful place,"

Indeed the house was a showpiece. It was a huge log home two stories in the center with a single story room off each end. The logs were stained a honey blonde and the roof was dark green steel. There was a huge wrap-around porch bordering the entire house. Off to the side was a three car garage made of the same logs with the same roof.

"This is a palace," Trevor said.

They pulled up to the driveway and parked and got out. As they walked up to the front porch a tall gray haired man opened the door and greeted them. He was lean and weathered looking with a friendly face and deep blue eyes.

"You must be Alfred's grandson and his friend," he said shaking hands.

"I'm Andy, his grandson and this is my friend Trevor, Mr.

Standish," Andy said.

"So your grandpa tells me you have a surprise for me," he said.

"Yes I think you'll be surprised," Trevor said.

"Have a seat and I'll go in and get some lemonade and we can chat here on the porch."

The boys sat in some comfortable deck chairs and the man returned with three glasses of lemonade.

"Ok, so your grandpa said you wanted to explore the caves at Bogus Bluff," Mr. Standish said. "Does your coming here mean you actually found something?"

The boys could hardly hold back their grins.

"Have you ever been in the tunnels?" Andy asked.

"Oh many times... my kids explored those tunnels for years, and I've been in them several times, but we never found a darn thing."

"We looked all through them too," Trevor said. "And we had the same conclusion, except that we found a half dollar."

"Well, that's more than I found," Standish said.

"Well then we began thinking," Andy said. "We wondered why the tunnel with the room only went a little way in and then stopped. Gramps told us that the tunnels were formed thousands, maybe millions of years ago when a sink hole up on the hill gathered acid rain that seeped down and ate away the limestone, creating the tunnels."

Standish leaned forward. "Go on."

Trevor was grinning. "We went up on the hill and looked and looked and we finally found a depression in the middle of a big briar patch. There was a pile of stones in the bottom that didn't seem natural and we dug around and found an opening hidden under a slab of stone."

Mr. Standish was listening with wide eyes.

"So we found the upper end of that tunnel that leads to the room. It's been blocked off from the topside by somebody who wanted to make people think that was the end of the tunnel."

Standish looked at them and said, "You know as many times as I was in that cave it never occurred to me that the tunnel leading off that room might have been blocked. So are you telling me....?"

Andy nodded. "We found it Mr. Standish... we found the gold from the American Trading Company."

Trevor got up and trotted over to the jeep and returned with one of the pillow cases they'd divided the coins into. They'd put three of them in the freezer and brought one to show Mr. Standish. Trevor grinned and turned the pillow case over and poured eighteen hundred gold coins on the glass top table they were sitting by.

Standish sat there speechless. He looked up at the boys. Then he picked up a coin and looked at it.

"My God, it's an 1812 French Bonapart and it's as new as the day it was minted."

"There are eighteen hundred of them in this pile," Trevor said.

"Eighteen hundred! Boy's you're rich!"

Andy laughed out loud. "Mr. Standish this is only one bag, we have three more at home. There are over seven thousand of these coins all together."

Standish sat there dumbfounded. "I never in all my life really believed in that story, but here is the proof that it really was true."

"We want to share our luck with you. If you hadn't given us permission we'd never have found it."

"Boys that is mighty generous of you but as you can see I'm pretty well taken care of. I've made a lot of money in my life and my wife and I live quite comfortably. I have two sons and a daughter and they're all very successful too. So even though you're very generous, I really can't accept any of this. You boys were clever enough to figure out the secret where many others failed, including my self. You deserve the treasure."

"Mr. Standish, you don't understand, these coins are worth

between $300 and $350 each. We have between two and two and a half million dollars depending on the exact price of the coins and the price of gold."

"Wait, I have to show my wife," Standish said and got up and went into the house. He returned with his wife. He explained about the boys and the treasure and she too was nearly speechless.

"She held a handful of the coins and asked Andy, "So what are your plans for all of this?"

"We're thinking of keeping it quiet and then helping people who need some help, using some for college and then we're not sure."

"So you're not just going to blow it?"

"No ma-am we're going to do some good with it."

She turned to her husband, "We don't need any more money, but what if we took a few of these coins and put them away for each of our grandchildren. Wouldn't that be a nice surprise someday for each of them?"

Standish nodded. "That's a great idea... if it's acceptable to the boys."

"How many grandchildren do you have?" Trevor asked.

"We have six, four boys and two girls."

Andy looked at Trevor and they seemed to know what each other were thinking.

"There are 1,800 coins here. That'd be 300 for each of them. That would be a gift to each of them of about a hundred thousand dollars."

"Oh that's too much, they don't need that much," Standish said. "We were just thinking of a few for each of them so they could show them off and tell their friends that this was treasure buried on their grandparents land."

"Mr. Standish, we have three more bags. This is fine with us. Just think of the look on those grandkids faces when they grow up and you hand each of them a bag full of gold."

"That would be something to see wouldn't it mother?"

Standish said to his wife.

"That is would father, that would be a wonderful thing."

"They'd each have enough money for the best education money could buy," Trevor suggested.

"Well ok then, and thank you boys. You could have kept the whole bunch and we'd have never been the wiser for it," Standish said.

"We'd have known and I don't think we'd have felt very good about it," Trevor said.

They all shook hands and Mrs. Standish hugged the boys and went inside to return with a sack of fresh baked cookies. "Here, she said, the most expensive cookies you'll ever eat."

Chapter 47

"That felt good," Andy said as they drove out of the Standish yard."

Trevor nodded. "Those grandkids will crap themselves when they see that pile of gold. How much cash do we still have?"

"Lots, there's more than $800 left from those first three coins we sold. What do you want?"

"I was thinking we'd go and get some new fishing lures and I need a spool of new line."

Andy grinned. "I think we can afford that."

They drove back to Andy's and he ran in and got the stash of cash and they drove to Walmart to shop. Since they had plenty of money they both bought a spool of line, the special expensive super braid kind, and about a dozen lures for the river. They picked up a small cooler and some pop and sub sandwiches and proceeded to the checkout line.

They were talking about where to go fishing that evening when they noticed a young woman with a small boy and a young man, barely older than they were who came into the line behind them. The young man had a "high and tight" haircut and was wearing military fatigue pants and an olive drab tee shirt.

The woman seemed stressed and the little boy was begging for some of the candy trinkets they always have at the checkout. The woman kept taking the stuff from him and telling him they

186

couldn't afford it.

"I'm not sure we have enough for the groceries honey," she said quietly to the boy. "If we have some left over you can have it."

The little boy began to cry and Andy turned to Trevor and they had one of those unspoken conversations.

Andy turned to the soldier. "Um, I see you're in the army," he said.

The guy nodded. "Yeah, I just got back from Iraq a week ago."

The little kid was still crying and Andy picked up the candy toy he had been after and said, "My friend and I just came into some money and we'd like to buy this for your son, if it's ok."

"Oh you don't have to....he'll be alright without it."

"I'm sure he will but we'd like to help out. In fact we'd like to pay for your groceries."

The girl looked surprised. "You can't possibly afford to pay for all of that," she said gesturing to the full cart.

"Believe me we can." Trevor said.

"Just put it on the belt with our stuff. Please, we'd really like to do it," Andy said.

The stunned couple stood there while Andy and Trevor helped them pile their groceries and other stuff on the belt. Trevor grabbed the bag with their fishing gear and food and then they helped them re-load their stuff back into the cart.

"The total is $358.53," the checkout girl said.

Andy peeled off 18, twenty dollar bills and handed them to her. She made the change and gave it back to him.

The young couple walked out with them looking quite stunned. They stopped by the couple's car. "We don't know how to thank you," the young man said.

Andy and Trevor shook hands with him. "Listen, we're the ones who should thank you for all you do. We got lucky and we're happy to share with you. In fact," Andy said, "take this and buy something nice for your wife and son." He handed the kid ten twenty dollar bills.

The girl hugged them both and had tears in her eyes. "You two are angels," she said.

They laughed. "I know a couple of moms who'd disagree with you," Trevor said.

"And a guy named Voldemort," Andy laughed.

The couple looked confused.

"Inside joke," Trevor said. The couple and the little boy thanked them again and they walked over and got into Trevor's jeep and drove out of the parking lot.

"That felt good," Andy said.

Trevor nodded. "I think we know now what we can do with all that money."

"Definitely."

Chapter 48

"Have you ever looked at EBay?" Trevor asked as they drove toward home.

"I've looked on it but never really looked into selling or buying something. I never had anything to sell or any money to buy."

Trevor laughed. "Me either. I think we should look at it and find out how it works. Then we can take a coin or two now and then and sell them to get cash to finance our projects."

"Projects?"

"Yeah, we've got a couple of million dollars in gold coins. There're not many places that we can spend them. So we need to turn them into currency. If we do it a little at a time we'll fly under the radar of any crook like our friend in Madison and we'll have cash when we need it. Plus I think you're pretty anonymous on EBay."

"That's a good idea. Rather than take them to a dealer and get cheated, we can sell them to the highest bidder and get what they're really worth. Let's go fishing tonight and camp on the river and then tomorrow we'll look at it and get it set up," Andy said.

They went home and hooked onto the boat, stopped and bought some night crawlers and pop and ice and headed out to the river. They fished several areas casting their new lures at likely looking spots and caught several nice smallmouth bass and walleye.

They moved in below a nice sandbar and were casting the lower end of it when Trevor set the hook on a fish. He began to reel and soon it was apparent that he was snagged and not hooked into a fish.

"Dang I just bought that lure," he said pulling on the line.

"So what? We've got a whole bag of them." Andy said.

"Yeah, but we paid almost $5 for that and I only got to use it for a few minutes," Trevor said grumpily.

Andy shrugged. "What can we do about it?"

Trevor laid his rod in the bottom of the boat and began taking off his clothes.

"What the heck are you doing?"

"I'm going in after it. It's brand new."

"Trev, it's $5, we have lots of $5 bills."

"I don't care. It's the principle of the thing. I only got to throw it a couple of times."

He stripped naked and let himself over the side of the boat. "Whooie, the water's cold," he said.

Andy just shook his head.

Trevor followed the line and took a deep breath and dove. His bare butt was the last thing Andy saw as he disappeared under the water. Soon his feet came up and he kicked to keep himself down on the bottom. He was down quite a long time and finally he came up and gasped a big breath of air.

"Hee haw," he said holding up his new lure and a second one he'd gotten from the bottom. "There is a root down there and I not only got mine, but I got another one that somebody else lost. I think there are more, here take these, I'm going back."

He tossed the two lures into the boat and disappeared again. A minute later he re-appeared and had another lure and a jig in his hand. He had a huge grin on his face.

"You're one crazy person," Andy said laughing.

"You have no idea," Trevor said as he swam to the sandbar.

He crawled out on the sand and Andy pulled the anchor and drove the boat over and up onto the sand next to him.

"Are you getting in?" he said to his naked friend.

"Why don't we just camp here?" Trevor asked. "It's a good drop-off for fishing once it settles down again, there's fire wood not far away," he said pointing to the shore and a dead tree lying on the ground, "and I'm getting hungry."

"Ok, sounds good to me."

Andy got out and they pulled the boat up so it wouldn't float away. Then Andy stripped and they took a good swim. They dried off and put on their shorts and gathered wood for the evening fire. Then they sat and enjoyed their sandwiches and food and baited up to fish with crawlers.

They were sitting on the edge of the sandbar and the sun was just beginning to set in the west.

"When I was a kid, my dad would take me fishing in the evenings, and when the sun got down like that, almost to the river, he'd always tell me to listen to the hiss it made when it went into the water," Andy said.

Trevor grinned. "And I bet you thought you heard it."

Andy nodded. "I always said I heard it but I wasn't sure. I told Dad I did to make him happy. The sun had dipped lower and was an orange ball right on the horizon. A minute later it seemed to touch the water. Andy turned his ear to the west. "Listen... did you hear that?"

Trevor smiled at his best friend. "Yeah, I did."

Chapter 49

The boys fished until about ten o'clock and then stripped down to their boxers and climbed into their sleeping bags in their little pup tent. They lay in the tent with the light from the fire dancing on the side illuminating the inside enough to see each other.

"Today was a good day," Trevor said.

"Yeah it sure was. It's not every day you give six hundred thousand dollars away."

Trevor nodded. "But it was only right to share with Mr. Standish. If he hadn't allowed us to search the cave wouldn't have found the gold. But sharing our good fortune with that soldier and his family....that was a good thing."

"Yeah, you're right about that."

They lay there for a few minutes and then Andy said, "What do you think we should do about telling our parents? I mean, they're going to wonder if we buy something one of these days."

"Yeah, I agree, unless we decide not to spend any money on ourselves, we'll have to tell them. Plus they don't have to worry about a college fund anymore either. We need to tell them that too."

"I think they'll be ok with it, at least I hope so," Andy said.

"Maybe we can have your Gramps help us."

"That's a good idea we'll have to talk to him."

"Well, I'm getting sleepy," Trevor said.

"Good night, see you in the morning," Andy said.

Andy lay awake and soon he heard Trevor's breathing slow

down. The fire was just a glow on the tent and he could hear the river gurgling as it swept past the sandbar. Somewhere out in the current he heard the splash of a fish rising for a bug on the water and to the shore side he could hear a bullfrog croaking. He had a smile on his face as he drifted off to sleep.

The sun was shining on the tent making the inside quite warm when Trevor woke. He yawned and stretched and farted and Andy woke up laughing.

"Jeez, you're a pig," he said chuckling.

"Sorry, it slipped."

They both laughed and then they got out of their sleeping bags and walked to the edge of the sandbar and peed into the river. Andy took a stick and stirred the fire but it was pretty much gone.

"Well, I'm ready for breakfast and we ate everything we had with us, so I suggest we head for home and some vittles," Trevor said.

And that's what they did.

After breakfast they went on the internet and checked out EBay. They found out about making an account and decided that it was a good thing to do to try to sell some of the coins.

"Ok, we need a name," Andy said.

"How about Astor Trading?" Trevor said.

"Sure, for John Jacob Astor who owned the American Trading Company, good idea," Andy said.

They typed in the name and then added address and all the other information, got a password and then they had to get a PayPal account so they could get their money if they made a sale. It took another few minutes to set up the PayPal account.

They went on EBay and looked at coins for sale and saw a French Bonapart 20 Franc coin from 1834 that was in pretty poor condition. It was being bid on at that moment and it was at $342.

"Ours are a lot nicer than that," Trevor said.

"No kidding. We have to get a coin and take a picture of it on both sides to show how nice they are. Then we can put it on there and call it un-circulated since they really never were in circulation."

They took two coins, and put one head side up and the other backside up and took a digital picture of them. Then they went through the process of putting it up for bid. Once they had all the particulars filled in, they hit the button to open the bids.

"Ok, so we'll see if we get a buyer and how much they're really worth," Trevor said.

It took a few minutes and they refreshed the page and there was their coin.

"This is pretty exciting," Andy said.

"I wonder how long it'll take for a bid?" Trevor added.

He'd no more than said that and a bid of $250 appeared below the coin.

They looked at each other.

"Holy smokes that didn't take long," Andy said.

The bid box blinked and the number $275 appeared.

They looked at each other. "This is way cool," Andy said.

Chapter 50

The boys stopped to see Andy's grandparents and talked with his grandpa about telling their parents. He thought it was a good idea and said he'd invite everyone over for a barbeque on Sunday and that they'd break the news to them then. That seemed like a good plan to the boys.

They were still on the work schedules at their workplaces, so they both spent the next 8 hours doing their jobs. While it seemed kind of silly to work for $7.50 per hour when they had nearly two million dollars stashed away, they wanted to keep their lives as much the same as they had been.

After work they checked EBay and found their coin had a bid of $358.

"Holy smokes... that went up fast," Trevor said.

"That it did. We've got a little over 12 hours on the bid clock so we'll see if it climbs any farther."

The next morning the bid was at $375 and it stayed there until the bid clock ran out. They received an email telling them the email address of the winning bidder so Trevor mailed him to set up the shipping address and costs.

The return email came within ten minutes and the bidder was in Montana and asked if they had only the one coin or if they had any more. Trevor mailed back that they had more and asked him how many he wanted.

The return email said he'd take 10 coins if they had them.

"Wow, that's $3,750," Andy said.

"I'll tell him to put it in our PayPal account and we'll ship them for free," Trevor said.

Andy nodded in agreement.

By two hours time their account had the money in it. They

went to the store and bought some padded envelopes and wrapped the coins individually and put them inside. They took it to the post office and sent it Priority Mail and insured it for $4,000.

As they walked out of the post office, they were grinning from ear to ear.

"I think we should do something for Gramps," Andy said.

Trevor nodded in agreement. "He went through a lot of crap because of our gold exploring adventures. Although I think he enjoyed it. We should do something nice for him."

They went back to Andy's and went online and found a cruise ship with a great package price for a ten day cruise through the Bahamas. They booked it for two weeks from that weekend. Then they went to a beachwear site and got one more item.

Sunday came and the two families gathered at Gramps' house for a big cookout. After they'd all eaten and were well satisfied, Gramps got everyone's attention and started out to let them in on the big secret.

"I know you all are aware of the stories about Bogus Bluff and the gold treasure up there. Well a while back Andy and Trevor came and asked me about it and I gave them the full lecture, including the part about the story was probably just that... a story. Well the boys decided to find out for themselves and they were cleverer than hundreds of people have been over the last two hundred years. He turned to the boys who had brought one of the pillow cases full of coins with them. Andy got up and turned the pillow case over onto the picnic table and 1,800 gold coins spilled out into a glittering pile.

The parents were open mouthed. The questions started at a rapid rate and it took half an hour to get it all explained.

Gramps brought up the idea of keeping it secret and that it was going to be used for a lot of good, plus the best college educations money could buy for the boys. There was a lot of discussion about that but in the end the parents agreed to keep it to themselves.

"We've already shared with Mr. Standish," Andy said. "We gave him $600,000 for his six grandkids. And we helped a soldier buy a cartload of groceries and gave him some cash too. We want to help people anonymously who have troubles. We're not going to blow it on toys, but there might be a few trinkets in our future too," he said with a twinkle in his eye.

They all began to chat and talk about how clever the boys were and Andy and Trevor went to Trevor's jeep and came back with a package. They walked up to Gramps and handed it to him. On top was an envelope and he opened it first.

He looked at the tickets for the flight to Miami and the cruise to the Bahamas.

"What is this? I've never been on an airplane in my life and I'm not sure I want to start now."

"You will start now you old goat," Andy's grandma said looking over the cruise brochure. "Or I'll find some young 50 year old to accompany me."

Grandpa decided he would indeed go on the trip. Then he opened the box and held up a hot pink speedo.

"The chicks will dig you in that Gramps," Andy said laughing.

The old man grinned. "I'm going into the house and put it on and model it for you."

There was a chorus of NOs.

Chapter 51

When the boys got back to Andy's house they found an email from the buyer of their coins. He was ecstatic about the quality of them and wondered if they'd consider a larger purchase at a reduced price. They talked it over and decided to offer him 3 coins for $1000 if he took at least 30 coins at a time.

Within three minutes they had a reply: "Will put $10K in your PayPal account. When it is confirmed send the coins. I expect to have more orders in the near future for more if the price holds."

They emailed back and said they'd keep the offer open for him.

"This is great," Andy said. "We don't have to mess around with EBay every day and we can store up a little nest egg for future projects. If this guy gets full of coins we can start selling on EBay again."

They got the 30 coins ready to ship and the money appeared in their account, so they mailed the coins.

"I think we should spend the night on the river," Trevor said.

"We've got T-Bone steaks on sale right now at the grocery store. How about we get a couple of big steaks and take some potatoes to bake in the fire and celebrate?"

Andy thought that was a great idea so they got their gear together and an hour later they were sitting on the sandbar across from Bogus Bluff fishing with their feet in the water, and their potatoes wrapped in foil sitting next to the fire pit.

"It seems like ages ago we saw that opening and started this adventure," Trevor said looking up at the front opening to the cave.

"If you'd have told me that we'd end up with two million dollars worth of gold when we started talking about that place, I'd have thought you'd been hit in the head by a baseball and gone daffy."

"We're pretty darn lucky," Trevor said.

"Yeah, that's true but we did manage to figure out the secret where hundreds before us missed the clues."

"Well, at any rate, I wouldn't have wanted to have this adventure with anyone else but you," Trevor said.

Andy put his arm around Trevor's shoulder. "I feel the same pal.

They caught a few fish and turned them loose. Then Andy squeezed one of the potatoes and it was soft so they put an iron grate over the fire and laid their two huge T-Bones on it. The steaks began to sizzle and soon they began to smell wonderful. The boys got out plates and the extras like butter and salt and pepper and in about twelve minutes they took the steaks off the grill and put one on each plate. They each cut open a potato and slathered it with butter and sat back and ate.

"Mmmm, wow," Andy said.

"I agree," Trevor laughed.

The sun was just going down as they cleaned up their plates. They lay back in the sand and watched it as it touched the river in the west.

"I heard it that time," Trevor said.

Andy smiled. "Me too."

"You know," Trevor said. "We should go up there and let that slab down and seal that tunnel up. Some animal could fall down it or even a person. We need to take the come-along back too."

"Yeah, you're right, I forgot about the come-along. My boss

will be mad if I don't return it. Let's do it in the morning."

They sat by the fire and talked about things they'd like to do with some of the money. One idea was to take a coin or two to a different church each Sunday and drop them into the collection basket.

"How about when they sell Poppies? We could buy a Poppy and drop in a coin without them knowing?" Trevor said.

"And those Free Will Offerings at the Legion and Kiwanis, when they have pancake breakfasts, we can do it there too."

They planned on lots of places where they could give without being found out and the more they talked the more fun it became.

Finally they began to yawn and they turned in. They stripped down to their boxers and crawled into the tent. It didn't take long and they were both sound asleep.

Chapter 53

I n the morning they stirred the coals and soon had a breakfast fire going. They had brought bacon and eggs and in no time they were eating a hearty breakfast. After breakfast they took a bottle of shampoo and a bar of soap and took a bath in the river. They dried off and dressed and cleaned up their camp.

"Ok, let's go get that come-along," Andy said.

They motored across the river and tied the boat up to a tree and climbed up over the bank, crossed the highway and hiked up their trail.

"You should have seen old Voldemort when he ran down this trail after I doused him with the fire ants," Trevor said chuckling.

"He looked like one of those skinny things you see at a gas station with air blowing up making it fly all over the place, all arms and legs. I thought he'd lose it for sure and tumble all the way but he kept his feet going pretty fast. I almost felt sorry for him, but not quite."

They got to the briar patch and Andy said, "You know, let's go down one more time and just check around. We've got nothing else to do. I'd like to check the mud floor of that skinny tunnel. We didn't look at that very good. I doubt there's anything there but at over $300 a coin, I'd hate to leave any behind."

"It's ok with me. I never went in that tunnel anyway. Let's go."

They'd left their head lamps in the briar patch inside one of the ice cream pails with a lid so they had lights. They climbed down one by one and Andy led the way into the narrow tunnel.

"I just crawled through this that last time," he said over his shoulder. "I really didn't look around at all."

"Well, we'll keep our eyes pealed then," Trevor answered.

They crawled along slowly scraping away the now dry dirt

with their hands looking for any sign of coins. They were nearly half was in when Trevor said, "Hey, here's one."

He held up the coin and Andy could just make it out over his shoulder.

"Your foot pushed it to the surface," Trevor said. "I'm gonna look a little more right here where I found it."

Andy moved on and soon came to the drop where the tunnel went down into the hill. He scratched around a little and found nothing. Then he began to back up.

"Find any more?" Andy asked as he got to where he could see Trevor's light behind him.

"Yeah, one more."

Let's go back out and think this over," Andy said.

They backed out of the narrow tunnel and then took turns crawling up the rope to the surface.

"So what do you think?" Andy asked.

"I don't know. Do you suppose there are sacks of them hidden in that tunnel or maybe in the hole at the end?"

"Could be, but why would they divide them up like that?"

Trevor shrugged. "I don't have a clue," he said as he reached into his pocket and pulled the two coins out.

"What?" Trevor exclaimed.

"What's wrong?" Andy asked.

Trevor handed him the coins. Andy looked at them and then up at Trevor.

"These are different. C A R O L III 1788 on the front and D G H I S P. R. on the back. HISP, do you know what that is Trev?"

"That's what Spain called itself in those days...Hispania."

"Trev, these are Spanish Doubloons!"

10 Years Later
from the Milwaukee Journal/Sentinal

Golden Angel Strikes Again!

The unknown person dubbed the Golden Angel is once again making an appearance at local charities. Ten years ago seven gold coins were anonymously dropped into donation pails of the Salvation Army during the Christmas season. This practice continued every year and expanded to include many other charities.

After that first year, coins began to appear in the donation baskets of several churches and in the Free Will Offering boxes at many charities. The Salvation Army donations expanded to sites in many Wisconsin cities as well as cities in Iowa, Illinois, and Minnesota. The coins are 20 Franc French Bonaparte coins from 1812 and Spanish Doubloons minted in the late 1700's. Present value of the coins is estimated at about $350 each.

To date the largest donation has been to a church that had a devastating fire six years ago. The services for the church were being held in the local school gym until the church could be repaired and church officials found 100 of the coins in the collection basket after the service.

"No one knows who this person is," said Sister Mary Henry of St. John's Parish, "but he or she is truly an angel, a golden angel."

It has been suggested that the coins are coming from a person who is retired and has a huge fortune that he or she wants to share before his death. The mystery though is that in some locations, there have been watchers looking for such a person but no one has been seen that fits the bill.

"It seems that somehow, this person drops a coin into the pot and no one notices. We feel very blessed that this generous person shares his wealth with us. A lot of good comes from each of those coins," said Major Thomas Bell of the Salvation Army.

Just last week a soup kitchen in Milwaukee found ten of the coins in its donation box. "That's a lot of meals we can serve now," said Ophelia Randall, a volunteer at the kitchen.

Whoever the Golden Angel is, he's pretty slick, and very much appreciated. "When you see all the ugly things in the world that happen, something like this really makes you believe in the good that is out there," said Sister Henry.

The national charity, Wounded Warriors recently received a package containing about $75,000 worth of the coins. This charity helps returning veterans with wounds received in the war in Afghanistan.

So, whoever he may be he seems to have a huge supply of golden coins. Where he got them, nobody knows, but for those who have been helped by this generous person, they know they've been touched by a true angel.

Author's note:

Bogus Bluff is a real place and the caves are much as they are described in this book. Many years ago as a teenager I crawled through them with some friends and little did I know then that our little adventure would be a part of one of my books.

The caves and hill are on private property. Years ago people climbed up and searched the caves all the time but now days, thoughts of lawsuits and injuries have put a halt to that. The climb up the hill is very dangerous. So please respect the owner's privacy and do not try to explore without permission.

About the author:

Dan Bomkamp has made his home in the Wisconsin River valley all his life with the exception of his college years in La Crosse. He has been an avid hunter and fisherman his whole life. For many years he was in the sporting goods industry and began writing in the 80s for outdoor magazines. He is active in the Foreign Exchange Student program having hosted 33 boys from 13 countries over the years. Golden Retrievers have also been a big part of his life. He had at least one Golden sharing his home for 33 years. He lives in Muscoda with his cat, Tigger and his Boston Terrier, Buster.

Check out his website at www.danbomkamp.com

Or you can email him: danbomkamp@live.com